The Moonstone

Wilkie Collins

OXFORD
UNIVERSITY PRESS

OXFORD
UNIVERSITY PRESS

Oxford University Press is a department of the University of Oxford.
It furthers the University's objective of excellence in research, scholarship,
and education by publishing worldwide in

Oxford New York

Athens Auckland Bangkok Bogotá Buenos Aires Cape Town
Chennai Dar es Salaam Delhi Florence Hong Kong Istanbul Karachi
Kolkata Kuala Lumpur Madrid Melbourne Mexico City Mumbai
Nairobi Paris São Paulo Shanghai Singapore Taipei Tokyo Toronto Warsaw

with associated companies in Berlin Ibadan

Oxford is a registered trade mark of Oxford University Press

Illustrated by K. Y. Chan

Syllabus designer: David Foulds

Text processing and analysis by Luxfield Consultants Ltd

ISBN 0 19 585462 4

Printed in Hong Kong
Published by Oxford University Press (China) Ltd
18th Floor, Warwick House East, Taikoo Place, 979 King's Road, Quarry Bay
Hong Kong

THE MOONSTONE

The *Oxford Progressive English Readers* series provides a wide range of reading for learners of English.

Each book in the series has been written to follow the strict guidelines of a syllabus, wordlist and structure list. The texts are graded according to these guidelines; Grade 1 at a 1,400 word level, Grade 2 at a 2,100 word level, Grade 3 at a 3,100 word level, Grade 4 at a 3,700 word level and Grade 5 at a 5,000 word level.

The latest methods of text analysis, using specially designed software, ensure that readability is carefully controlled at every level. Any new words which are vital to the mood and style of the story are explained within the text, and reoccur throughout for maximum reinforcement. New language items are also clarified by attractive illustrations.

Each book has a short section containing carefully graded exercises and controlled activities, which test both global and specific understanding.

CONTENTS

PROLOGUE

The history of the Diamond

Hundreds of years ago in India, an unusually large diamond called the Moonstone was set in the forehead of a statue of a Hindu god, and placed in a sacred temple. Legend says that three Hindu priests were commanded by the god himself to watch over the Diamond until the end of time. It was also said that misfortune would come to anyone else who touched it, and to his family.

In the eleventh century, thieves stole the Moonstone from the statue, and it passed from one owner to another. One by one the owners of the Moonstone died terrible deaths. And the three guardian priests kept their watch.

In the last years of the eighteenth century, the English army attacked and captured a city in India called Seringapatam. The ruler of Seringapatam was at that time the owner of the Moonstone. He was killed in the battle. An English officer, John Herncastle, who had heard the story of the Moonstone, decided to get the Diamond for himself. He entered the palace storeroom, and discovered three Indian priests keeping watch there. A struggle broke out, and Herncastle killed all three holy men. He quickly found the Diamond, and took it. As he turned to the door, his beautiful prize flashing in his hand, one of the priests gasped with his dying breath, 'The Moonstone will have its revenge!'

PART 1
The Loss of the Diamond (1848)
Told by Gabriel Betteredge, servant to Lady Verinder

THE THREE INDIANS

The family servant

This morning, my lady's nephew, Mr Franklin Blake, told
me that he and the lawyer, Mr Bruff, had decided to have
the whole story of Miss Rachel's lost Diamond written
5   down. It was agreed that the people who were most
closely connected with each part of the story should write
about what happened, as far as they knew it.

As a beginning, I will tell you that at the age of fifteen
I worked as a servant-boy to the three Herncastle sisters,
10   Miss Adelaide, Miss Caroline and Miss Julia, who was in
my opinion the best of all three. I lived with the Herncastle
family until Miss Julia married Sir John Verinder. She then
became Lady Verinder, and I went with her to her
husband's house and lands in Yorkshire, near Frizinghall.

15   After a time, I married my housekeeper (it seemed to
me it would be cheaper to marry her than to keep paying
her). After five years she died, leaving me a little girl,
Penelope. Shortly afterwards Sir John died, and my lady
was left with her daughter, Rachel. My lady was very good
20   to Penelope and me, and when my daughter was old
enough, she became Miss Rachel's personal maid. Not
long afterwards I became the chief servant in the whole
house.

Now I must tell you about the Diamond, beginning on
25   the day that we heard that Mr Franklin Blake was coming
to visit her ladyship and Miss Rachel.

Franklin Blake

On Wednesday morning, 24th May 1848, my lady had
some surprising news for me. Her nephew, Franklin
Blake, had come back from abroad (he had been in
Europe for some years, finishing off his education). He   5
would be staying for a month.

I remembered Master Franklin as a fine young lad, but
he had some bad habits, especially to do with money.
When I had last seen him, as a boy, he had borrowed
seven shillings from me. He was now twenty-five. I looked   10
forward to seeing what kind of man he had become.
However, I did not expect to get my seven shillings back.

Early the next morning, my lady and Miss Rachel drove
into town. I was busily checking to see that all was ready
for our guest's arrival that evening, when I heard a sound   15
like the beating of a drum. Going round to the front of
the house, I found three Indians there, dressed in white.
With them was a thin little English boy. When I asked
them what they wanted, they said they were travelling
magicians, and asked permission to perform their tricks   20
before the lady of the house. I informed them that she
was out. They bowed low, and went away.

I went to sit in the sun, but then my daughter Penelope
came along from the house. She wanted me to have the
Indians arrested at once. She said that they meant to harm   25
Mr Franklin! I was very surprised. At first I did not believe
her, but I could see that she was very serious about it, so
I listened. This is what she told me.

Penelope had been in the garden, and had seen the
Indians leaving the house. As there are a lot of trees in   30
the garden, and she was behind them, they did not see
her, but she could see them. Naturally, she wanted to
know what they were doing, so she watched them. After
they had walked a little way, they all turned and stared
hard in the direction of our house. Then the chief   35
Indian said (in English) to the boy, 'Hold out your hand.'

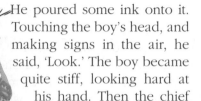

He poured some ink onto it. Touching the boy's head, and making signs in the air, he said, 'Look.' The boy became quite stiff, looking hard at his hand. Then the chief Indian said to him, 'Is it on this road and no other that the English gentleman from foreign parts will travel today?'

The boy nodded once. 'Has he got It with him?' The boy nodded again. 'Will he arrive, as he said, at the end of the day?' The boy said he was too tired to see any more. After that the strange group went on their way.

My girl and I both thought the 'Englishman from foreign parts' must be Mr Franklin, but what could 'It' be?

Rosanna Spearman

After Penelope went back into the house, the kitchen-maid came out, complaining that the new servant, Rosanna, was late for dinner. I said I'd go and find her.

I was fond of Rosanna Spearman. She had had an unhappy life. She was a child of the London streets, and had kept herself alive by stealing, until she was caught. Then she was sent to prison and after that, to a special school. My lady took her from the school, and gave her a chance to better herself. In return, Rosanna worked very hard to show that she deserved my lady's kindness.

Very few people knew where our new servant had come from, but even so the other servants did not like her. She was a quiet girl and did not make friends. She was also terribly plain-looking, and one of her shoulders was bigger than the other.

I thought I knew where I would find her. Our house is in the eastern part of Yorkshire, and close to the sea. There is a walk through a wood of fir trees which brings you out on the loneliest and ugliest little bay on all our coast. Small sand-hills run down to the sea here, and end in two stretches of rock which reach out opposite each other. One of these stretches of rock is called the North Spit, and one the South Spit. Between the two lies the most horrible quicksand on the shores of Yorkshire. If you step into it by mistake, that is the last mistake you will ever make. Slowly it will suck you down: nothing escapes, not even the strongest animals can get out once they have fallen in. When the tide turns, the whole surface of the quicksand shakes and trembles in the strangest manner. It is called the Shivering Sand. No sensible person ever likes to go anywhere near it, but for some reason, it was there that Rosanna could always be found.

When I reached the beach, there she was, all alone and looking out at the sea. She turned, and I saw that she was crying. She was still troubled by her past. I sat down beside her, and asked her why she came to this spot.

'I don't know,' she answered. 'I try to keep away from it, but I can't. I even dream of it. Sometimes I think that this place will one day be my grave. Look at the way it trembles,' she said. 'Isn't it wonderful? Isn't it terrible?'

Suddenly a voice shouted, 'Betteredge, where are you?'

Rosanna jumped to her feet. I was amazed to see her brighten all over with a kind of breathless surprise.

'Oh! Who is that?' she said softly.

Coming through the sand-hills was a very handsome young man with a happy smile on his face.

'Dear old Betteredge,' he said. 'Don't you know me?'

Here, four hours
before we expected him, was Mr Franklin Blake!

Rosanna's face went a deep red, and she suddenly
turned and left us without a word.

5   'What an odd girl!' said Mr Franklin, a little surprised.

The wicked Colonel's Diamond

Mr Franklin explained that he had a good reason for
coming early. He said he was sure that for the past three
days, someone had been following him. He had caught
10 the early morning train to escape his watcher. He had
already spoken to Penelope, who had told him about the
three Indians.

'I think that they may have something to do with the
man who has been following me,' said Mr Franklin. 'And
15 I believe that the "It" they were talking about means this.'
He pulled something out of his pocket. 'This, Betteredge,
is my uncle Herncastle's famous Diamond.'

'Good Lord, sir!' I said in amazement, 'what are you
doing with the wicked old Colonel's Diamond?'

20 'The Colonel is dead,' replied Mr Franklin, 'and he left
his Diamond as a birthday present to my cousin Rachel.
But why do you call him "the wicked Colonel"?'

I told Mr Franklin that many things were said about the
Colonel and his bad ways, but the story of the Diamond

was all I needed to mention. It was said that while he was in India, the Colonel had obtained a most wonderful diamond in a very disgraceful way. No one knew the full story, but they knew enough and they were happy to guess the rest. When John Herncastle came back to England, respectable society turned its back upon him, but he kept the Diamond in spite of this.

After his return to England from India, I saw him only once. He came to my lady's home in London. It was Miss Rachel's birthday, 21st June, and he told me he had come to wish her many happy returns of the day. However, my lady had never liked the Colonel. When I informed her that he had come to the house, she refused to allow him to see either herself or her daughter. I went back to tell the Colonel. I expected him to be angry, but if he was, he did not show it. Instead he looked at me for a moment, and laughed. 'I shall remember my niece's birthday,' he said.

The next birthday came round, and we heard that he was ill. Now, six months later, the Colonel was dead.

'Betteredge,' said Mr Franklin, 'we must ask ourselves three things. Was the Colonel's Diamond an object of evil in India? Has this evil followed the Diamond to England? Did the Colonel know that great misfortune would come to anyone who owned the Diamond, and has he left it to his niece knowing that it may harm her?' I could see that Mr Franklin's European education had turned him into a very clear thinker.

The Colonel's will

Mr Franklin continued.

'My uncle, the Colonel, had some family papers which my father wanted. When he returned from India, he said my father could have these papers if he would do something for him. The Colonel had decided that if he kept the Diamond himself, something very bad would happen to him. He wanted my father to take the Diamond and put it in a safe place. Every year he would send a letter to let my father know he was still alive. If no letter arrived, it would mean he had been murdered. In that case, my father was to open an envelope which contained instructions on what to do with the Diamond.

'Everything was agreed, and as soon as my father received the Diamond, he put it in a bank. Year after year the letters came. The last one arrived six months ago, saying that the Colonel was dying of natural causes. He asked my father to be the executor for his will. He left the Moonstone as a birthday present to his niece. After the Colonel's death, we found out that the Diamond was worth at least twenty thousand pounds.

'Although the Colonel was not murdered, my father was curious to know what instructions the mysterious envelope contained. When he opened it, he found a letter saying that if the Colonel died by an act of violence, the Diamond was to be cut up into four or six separate stones. These were to be sold, and the money given to a good cause. The Diamond cut up would in fact be worth far more than the Diamond whole.

'I believe my uncle's life was protected by this plan. The Colonel must have known that the Moonstone was only really important to some people if it was kept in one piece. If someone just wanted to take the Colonel's wealth, these instructions made murdering him an even better idea. But if there was a plot to get the whole Diamond for some other reason, and not for the money, then the Colonel was safe.'

'What plot do you speak of, sir?' I cried.

'A plot organized by the people who were the first owners of the Diamond,' said Mr Franklin. 'The Diamond belongs to one of their gods, and they will do anything to get it back.'

The Indian magicians! We looked at each other for a long moment.

MISS RACHEL'S BIRTHDAY PRESENT

Difficult questions

'Betteredge,' said Mr Franklin, 'we must now ask ourselves why the Colonel has left this Diamond to his niece. Here, read this.' He handed me a piece of paper on which was written a part of the Colonel's will. This is what it said:

I leave to my niece, Rachel Verinder, the yellow Diamond known as Moonstone, subject to this condition: that her mother shall be living at the time. The Diamond shall be given to my niece, on her next birthday after my death, and in the presence of my sister Julia Verinder. My sister should be told that I give the Diamond to her daughter to show that I have forgiven her for the way in which she has behaved towards me; and especially the insulting way in which I was treated when I last visited her house.

'By bringing the Diamond to Rachel, am I helping the Colonel to get his revenge, or am I showing that he was really a forgiving man?' asked Mr Franklin. 'How are we to explain why he wants to give Rachel the Diamond only if her mother is alive? Oh, what should I do?'

'Miss Rachel's birthday is on 21st June, which is nearly four weeks away,' I said. 'Let's wait and see what happens. If we need to, we can warn my lady when the time comes. And in the meantime, why not take the Diamond to the bank at Frizinghall? It will be quite safe there.'

Mr Franklin jumped to his feet. 'Betteredge,' he said, 'that is a very good idea. I shall go this minute.'

We found the fastest horse in the stables, and he rode away to put the Diamond once more in the bank.

Love at first sight

Penelope told me that after Rosanna had returned to the house, she asked hundreds of questions about Mr Franklin Blake, and had been seen writing his name inside her
5 sewing-box. She had also been crying and looking at her badly-shaped shoulder in the mirror.

'Father,' said Penelope, 'I think Rosanna has fallen in love with Mr Franklin at first sight!'

Mr Franklin returned from Frizinghall, having put the
10 Diamond safely into the bank. I did not see his meeting with his cousin, but Penelope said she had never seen Miss Rachel looking so pretty. When I took Mr Franklin his brandy, I found that the sight of Miss Rachel had made him forget about the Moonstone.

15 At midnight, I locked up, accompanied by Samuel, another servant. Then I stepped outside for a breath of fresh air. Looking along the path beside the terrace, I saw the shadow of a person at the corner of the house. I went back to get Samuel. We each took a gun, and went all
20 round the house, but found no one. As we returned, I noticed a small bottle lying on the ground, full of a thick, black ink. I realized that I had disturbed the three Indians.

Painting Miss Rachel's door

The next morning I showed Mr Franklin the little bottle,
25 and told him what had happened. He thought the Indians had brought the boy to the house to show them the way to the Diamond, and had discovered that it had been put in the bank. Mr Franklin and I waited to see what might happen, but the Indians seemed to have disappeared.

30 On 29th May, Mr Franklin and Miss Rachel together began to paint her sitting-room door with pictures of birds, flowers and fairies. It took a long time, but they never seemed to get tired of the work. We servants began to wonder if there might be a wedding in the house quite
35 soon. It was easy to see that Mr Franklin was in love.

But Miss Rachel was a girl who did not tell her secrets to anyone. No one was sure what her feelings were towards Mr Franklin.

I myself believed that Miss Rachel had chosen another cousin, Godfrey Ablewhite, to be her husband. He stood over six feet tall. He had a smooth face and golden hair. And he was not only handsome, but good too. He did a lot to help ladies' societies to collect money for the poor. His speeches at charity meetings were quite famous. What chance did Mr Franklin have against such a man as this? Well, we would find out at Miss Rachel's birthday party, when the two men met.

Meanwhile, Mr Franklin never stopped trying to please Miss Rachel. He even gave up smoking his cigars because she hated the smell, although he slept so badly afterwards that she begged him to start smoking once more.

Godfrey Ablewhite arrives

Rosanna's behaviour was very peculiar at this time. One day Penelope caught her in Mr Franklin's room, secretly removing a rose which Miss Rachel had given to him, and putting in another which she had picked herself. The poor girl was also rather rude to Miss Rachel, and was always getting in Mr Franklin's way.

On 20th June a note arrived from Mr Godfrey, saying that the next day, he and his sisters would ride over for dinner. He sent Miss Rachel a beautiful china box with his love and best wishes. Mr Franklin had only given her a

small, plain necklace. However, Penelope still thought that
Mr Franklin would win the love of Miss Rachel.

    The next day Mr Franklin rode over to Frizinghall to
collect the Moonstone from the bank. He met Mr Godfrey
and his sisters on the way back. They all arrived together,
late in the afternoon. Mr Godfrey did not seem to be very
happy, but his sisters more than made up for him. They
were big, yellow-haired, red-faced girls, who would laugh
and scream with excitement at the smallest thing.

    I asked Mr Franklin if he had the Diamond (he had),
and if he had seen the Indians (he had not). Then he
hurried off to find my lady. Penelope was sent to tell Miss
Rachel that Mr Franklin wished to see her.

The beautiful Diamond

Moments later, I heard a noise coming from the small
drawing-room. I went in to discover what was happening.
There stood Miss Rachel at the table with the Diamond
in her hand. The two Miss Ablewhites were
screaming with delight every time the jewel
flashed on them. At the opposite
end of the table stood Mr Godfrey,
clapping his hands, and singing
softly, 'Beautiful! Beautiful!'
Mr Franklin sat in a chair by
the bookcase, looking anxious.
And at the window stood my
lady, holding the piece of
paper with the Colonel's will
written on it, in her hand.
Then she asked me to
come to her room later,
and left, puzzled by
what she had read.
Miss Rachel turned to
me.

'Look, Gabriel,' she said, and flashed the Diamond before my eyes. Lord bless us! It was a beauty. Nearly as large as a bird's egg, and the colour of the harvest moon.

When I went to my lady's room, our conversation was similar to the one I had with Mr Franklin at the Shivering Sand, but I didn't tell her about the visit from the Indians. I could see she was worried enough about the Diamond, and did not want to make things worse.

Later, Penelope came to see me. She whispered, 'Miss Rachel will not marry Mr Godfrey! They went out laughing, arm in arm, to walk in the rose garden. They came back walking separately, as serious as could be, not looking at each other at all. "Let's forget what has passed, Godfrey," she said. He waited a little by himself. "Awkward!" he said, "very awkward!" So you see, Father, I'm sure Miss Rachel would rather have Mr Franklin!'

The dinner party

There were twenty-four for dinner. Among the guests were Mr Candy, our local doctor, and Mr Murthwaite, who was a famous world traveller. They sat on either side of Miss Rachel at dinner. She was wearing her wonderful birthday present pinned on her white dress.

Mr Murthwaite had been to India many times, and he was interested in the Moonstone, for he had often heard of it when he was there. After looking at it, he said,

'If you ever go to India, Miss Verinder, don't take your gift with you. A Hindu diamond is holy. It belongs to a god. I know a temple where the priests would kill you in order to get a diamond like that back.'

As the dinner went on, I noticed that it didn't seem to be as enjoyable as other parties we had had in the house. At times people said the most unfortunate things to one another, and sometimes no one had anything to say at all. Mr Godfrey Ablewhite, usually an interesting speaker, did nothing to help. He spent all his time talking quietly to his neighbour, Miss Drusilla Clack — a member of one of those ladies' societies — about his charity work.

Mr Franklin tried to keep the conversation going, but often he chose the wrong subject and offended a guest. For example, he talked about how badly he had been sleeping lately. Mr Candy immediately told him that he needed a course of medicine. Mr Franklin refused to believe him, and they argued about it. They got angrier and angrier, until my lady had to make them change the subject.

Dinner had just finished when there came the sound of an Indian drum from the terrace. So the Indians had followed the Moonstone to the house! I went out to send them away, but I was too late: the dinner guests were there before me. Miss Rachel stood in front of the Indians, with the Diamond gleaming on her dress!

The first thing I noticed was the sudden appearance of Mr Murthwaite. He came quietly behind the magicians and spoke to them in their own language. They turned on him as quick as tigers. The next moment, however, they were bowing low, and then Mr Murthwaite went away as silently as he had come. The chief Indian bowed to my lady, and told her that the performance was over. I went with them to the gate and made sure they left.

Mr Murthwaite

On my way back to the house, Mr Franklin called me. He was standing on the terrace with Mr Murthwaite.

'This is Gabriel Betteredge,' Mr Franklin said. 'He is an old servant and friend of the family. Tell him what you have just told me.'

'Mr Betteredge,' began Mr Murthwaite, 'I know what Indian magicians are really like. All you have seen tonight is a very bad imitation. Those men were Hindu priests. I accused them, and you saw what happened. They have done two things which Hindu priests should never do: they have left India, and they have disguised their true identities. They must have a very important reason for doing this. I believe they are trying to get the Moonstone back. They want to return it to the forehead of the statue. They are cruel men, Mr Betteredge, and they will stop at nothing to get what they want. If a thousand people stood between them and their Diamond, they would kill them all.'

'They have seen the Moonstone on Miss Verinder's dress,' said Mr Franklin. 'What can we do?'

'Do what your uncle Herncastle threatened to do,' answered Mr Murthwaite. 'Have the Diamond cut up. That will put an end to their plots for good.'

I went to my own room. After a while, Penelope came to see me. She had been serving tea. She had heard Mr Franklin having an argument about ladies' charities, with Mr Godfrey. Mr Candy, the doctor, had mysteriously disappeared from the drawing-room, and had then mysteriously returned and started talking to Mr Godfrey.

As our guests were leaving, it began to rain. Mr Candy had an open carriage, and I was afraid he would get wet through. But he told me not to worry. Doctors were used to the rain, he said. They had to go out in it so often!

STRANGE BEHAVIOUR

The Diamond disappears

When the last of the guests had gone, I went back into the hall. My lady and Miss Rachel came out of the drawing-room, followed by the two gentlemen.

5 'Rachel,' my lady asked, 'where are you going to put your Diamond?' Miss Rachel said that she would put it in an Indian cabinet which stood in her sitting-room.

'Come to my room first thing in the morning,' said my lady. 'I shall have something to say to you.' With those

10 words she left us.

Miss Rachel said good night to Mr Godfrey. Then she turned to Mr Franklin, with a smile. I began to think that Penelope might be right, and that Miss Rachel preferred him to Mr Godfrey.

15 Mr Franklin looked tired and worried as he took his candle to go upstairs. He asked me to send Samuel up to his room with some brandy-and-water, which I did.

Next morning, at half-past seven, I woke and got out of my bed. I was just going downstairs, when I heard

20 footsteps behind me. It was Penelope.

'Father!' she screamed. 'The Diamond is gone! Gone! Nobody knows how! Come and see.' She took my arm and pulled me after her into our young lady's sitting-room, which opened into her bedroom. Miss Rachel was

25 standing at her bedroom door. One of the drawers of the Indian cabinet had been pulled out as far as it would go.

'I myself saw Miss Rachel put the Diamond into that drawer last night!' whispered my daughter.

Miss Rachel glanced at me, and in a strange voice said:

30 'The Diamond is gone!'

Then she went into her bedroom and locked the door.

Mr Franklin calls the police

The news spread quickly through the house. Miss Rachel allowed my lady into her bedroom, but refused to come out herself. Mr Godfrey was shocked and didn't know what to do. Mr Franklin seemed to be as helpless as his cousin.

For once Mr Franklin had had a good night's sleep, but it seemed to have stopped his brains from working! However, after a cup of coffee he was back to normal. He ordered the servants to leave all the lower doors and windows exactly as they had been left when we locked up the night before. Then he sent Penelope to knock on Miss Rachel's door.

Lady Julia came out looking very puzzled and upset.

'The loss of the Diamond seems to have affected Rachel very strangely,' she said to Mr Franklin. 'She will not speak of it at all.'

'We must send for the police,' Mr Franklin replied. He thought that the Indians had certainly stolen the Diamond. He said that he would himself ride to Frizinghall with a letter from my lady asking for the police. She wrote the letter a little unwillingly. I believe it would have been a relief to her to allow the thieves to get away with the Moonstone.

I went out with Mr Franklin to the stables, and told him I could not see how the Indians could possibly have got into the house. I had looked round the house and found everything locked and bolted as I had left it the night before.

After breakfast I told my lady the whole story of the Indians, but she was far more worried about her daughter. The loss of the jewel seemed almost to have driven Miss Rachel mad.

A thief in the house

Mr Godfrey wandered around the house and gardens, looking as if he did not know where he was or what he was doing. I was nervous and bad-tempered. This trouble with the Moonstone had upset us all.

Just before eleven o'clock, Mr Franklin returned. He said that Chief Inspector Seegrave, of the local police, and two of his men were coming. But, he added, it was no use suspecting the Indians. They were innocent! All three had been seen returning to Frizinghall last night between ten and eleven o'clock. At midnight, the police had, for some reason, searched the house where they were staying, and they had all been there. Soon after midnight I myself had safely shut up the house. The local judge said he could keep them locked up for a week for begging, but he would have to let them go after that.

Ten minutes later Chief Inspector Seegrave arrived at the house. It was not long before he decided that the robbery must have been committed by someone in the house.

The Chief Inspector said the servants should come one by one to Miss Rachel's sitting-room, so that he might ask them some questions. All the women servants rushed upstairs at once. Each one thought she was under suspicion, and wanted to declare her innocence. With a stern look, he told them all to return downstairs. Suddenly he pointed to a mark on the painting on Miss Rachel's door, just under the lock.

'Look what one of your skirts has done!' he shouted. Rosanna Spearman, the nearest to the mark, left the room instantly. The others followed.

My daughter was sent for, as she had first discovered the robbery. She told the Chief Inspector that she had seen Miss Rachel put the Diamond in the drawer of the cabinet. She had gone in with Miss Rachel's cup of tea the next morning, and had found the drawer open and empty.

Miss Rachel refused to see the Chief Inspector. She said she had nothing to tell him. Mr Franklin and Mr Godfrey were asked what they knew about the robbery, but neither could help.

Then the bedroom door opened, and Miss Rachel came out.

'Where is Mr Franklin Blake?' she asked.

'Mr Franklin is outside, on the terrace, Miss,' I answered.

Without listening to the Chief Inspector, who tried to speak to her, she left the room, and went down to her cousin. What she said to him must have surprised him, judging by the expression on his face. While they were still talking together, my lady appeared on the terrace. Miss Rachel saw her, said a few last words to Mr Franklin, and suddenly went back into the house again, before her mother could talk to her. Soon after that Mr Godfrey joined them. Mr Franklin, I suppose, must have told them what had happened, for they both looked amazed and stood staring at him.

Miss Rachel walked quickly through to her bedroom, and turned on the Chief Inspector at her door. 'I have not sent for you!' she cried out angrily. 'My Diamond is lost. Neither you nor anybody else will ever find it!' With those words she went in, locked the door and burst out crying.

I was puzzled by my young lady's behaviour. Why was she so annoyed with Mr Franklin for having sent for the police? Why should she object to the police trying to find the thief and get the Diamond back? And how could she know that the Moonstone would never be found?

Rosanna speaks to Mr Franklin

Mr Seegrave asked me if any of the servants had known where the Diamond had been put for the night.

'I am sure that Samuel the footman, my daughter and
5　I knew,' I said. 'And for all I know, everyone else in the house may have known where it was.'

The Chief Inspector asked me if the servants could be trusted. I thought of Rosanna Spearman who had once been a thief. But the poor girl had shown no sign of
10　dishonesty since she had been working with us.

'All our people are honest, sir,' I said.

One after another they were questioned and proved to have nothing to say. Their rooms were searched, but the Diamond was not found.

15　I was sent for by Mr Franklin in the library. As I was about to enter, to my surprise, who should walk out through the library door, but Rosanna Spearman! The girl's face was red and she looked pleased with herself. When I entered the room, Mr Franklin asked for a carriage to
20　take him to the station.

'I want to send a telegram,' he said. 'My father knows the Chief of Police, and he can send us the right man to solve this mystery. Talking of mysteries,' he went on, 'I think Rosanna knows more about the Moonstone than she
25　should. She came in here with a ring I dropped. When I had thanked her, instead of going she stood at the table, looking at me in the oddest manner. "This is a strange thing about the Diamond, sir," she said. "They will never find it, sir, will they? No! nor the person who took it, I'm
30　sure of that!" She nodded and smiled at me. Before I could ask her what she meant, she turned and left the room!'

'I'll talk to my lady about it, sir,' I said. 'Maybe she can find out from Rosanna what it was all about.'

On my way to order the carriage, I looked in at the
35　servants' dining-room. Rosanna was not there. They said she had been taken ill, and had gone to her room.

'The poor thing is breaking her heart about Mr Franklin Blake,' said Penelope.

This, perhaps, was the reason for her strange behaviour. She may have just wanted Mr Franklin to speak to her.

When I went round to the front door with the carriage, I found Mr Franklin, Mr Godfrey and the Chief Inspector waiting. The Chief Inspector   10
thought that someone in the house must have been working with the Indians, and he was going to Frizinghall to question them. Mr Godfrey was going with him.

The day wore on. Miss Rachel stayed in her room. My lady was so upset that I decided not to worry her any   15
more by telling her what Rosanna had said to Mr Franklin.

Later, the two gentlemen came back from Frizinghall. Nothing could be found to connect the Indians with any of our servants.

Sergeant Cuff arrives   20

On Friday morning, we heard two pieces of news.

The baker said he had met Rosanna Spearman on the previous afternoon, with a thick veil over her face, walking towards Frizinghall. But Rosanna had spent all Thursday afternoon in her room!   25

The postman told us that Mr Candy, when he drove off in the rain after the party, had caught a bad cold, and was now very ill, poor man.

After breakfast a telegram came. A man called Sergeant Cuff would arrive by the morning train. I went to meet him myself. He was a thin, elderly man, with a face as sharp as a knife, and skin as dry as an autumn leaf.

5   At the house, after meeting my lady, the Sergeant asked to talk to Chief Inspector Seegrave in Miss Rachel's sitting-room. The Sergeant examined the cabinet and the sitting-room very carefully, asking questions all the time. At last he reached the door, and pointed to the mark which Chief
10   Inspector Seegrave had already noticed. He asked how it happened, and we told him the story. Sergeant Cuff turned to the Chief Inspector.

'Did you notice whose dress did it?' he asked.

The Chief Inspector had to admit that he had no idea.

15   'We must see the dress that made that mark,' said Sergeant Cuff, 'and we must know for certain when that paint was wet. What time was it when the servants were in here yesterday morning? Eleven o'clock? Is there anybody who knows whether the paint was wet then?'

20   ## 'Don't allow Mr Franklin to help you!'

In half a minute, Mr Franklin was in the room.

'The paint dries in twelve hours,' he told the Sergeant. 'That was the last bit of the door to be painted. We had finished it by three o'clock on Wednesday afternoon.'

25   'Today is Friday,' said Sergeant Cuff. 'At three o'clock on Wednesday afternoon, that painting was completed. The paint dried by three o'clock on Thursday morning. At eleven o'clock on Thursday that paint had been dry for eight hours. I think you may have given us just the help
30   we were looking for, Mr Franklin.'

At these words, the bedroom door opened, and Miss Rachel appeared: 'Did you say that he had given you the help?' she asked, pointing to Mr Franklin.

'It is possible, Miss,' said the Sergeant, looking at her
35   closely.

'Do your job by yourself, and don't allow Mr Franklin Blake to help you!' She said those words hatefully and savagely.

'Thank you, Miss,' said the Sergeant. 'Do you happen to know anything about the mark on the door?'

'I know nothing about the mark,' she answered, and turning away, she once more locked herself into her bedroom. We could hear her crying again. Mr Franklin looked very upset.

'Miss Verinder appears to be a little bad-tempered about the loss of her Diamond,' remarked the Sergeant. 'Now, the next thing to find out is when the paint was last seen without the mark. Who was the last person in the room on Wednesday night?'

'Miss Rachel, I suppose, sir,' I said.

'Or perhaps your daughter,' said Mr Franklin to me. He explained that my daughter was Miss Verinder's maid.

'Ask your daughter to come here,' said the Sergeant.

Penelope gave her evidence. She had noticed the surface as late as twelve o'clock at night when she had wished her young lady good night. She had been very careful not to touch it. She fetched the dress she had worn that night; there was no paint stain on it.

Someone must have been into the room and taken the jewel, between midnight and three o'clock on Thursday morning.

'Well now,' said the Sergeant, 'we must find out whether there is any clothing in this house with paint on it. Second, we must find out who that clothing belongs to. Third, we must find out how that person came to be in this room, between midnight and three o'clock in the morning.' He said to Chief Inspector Seegrave, 'I'll work on this alone from now on.'

THE HIDING-PLACE

The search

My lady arrived, and the Sergeant told her what he had discovered. He asked her if he could search for the clothing with the paint on it. She agreed.

5   Mr Godfrey was going to London that day, but when he heard of the search, he at once gave the keys of his suitcase to Sergeant Cuff.

'My luggage can follow me to London,' he said.

Mr Franklin was going with his cousin to the station.
10   He told the Sergeant that he could search his wardrobe.

'Before we begin,' said Sergeant Cuff, 'I want to know that all the clothes are here. If there is something missing, it may well have the paint on it. It might have been sent to be washed, or it might have been taken away.'

15   The laundry-book was then brought in by Rosanna Spearman. Sergeant Cuff looked closely at her.

'The last time I saw her,' he said, 'she was in prison.'

'She has been most honest since she came to work here,' said my lady.

20   My lady went into Miss Rachel's room to get her keys, but Miss Rachel refused to have her wardrobe examined.

'Ah!' said the Sergeant. 'Then we must give up the search.'

'What's to be done next?' I asked.

'Come out into the garden,' said Sergeant Cuff, 'and let's
25   have a look at the roses.'

Rosanna hides in the bushes

We went out into the garden and started walking.

'Did you notice anything strange in any of the servants after the loss of the Diamond?' the Sergeant asked. 'Was
30   any one of them taken ill?'

I had just remembered Rosanna's sudden illness at dinner yesterday, when I saw the Sergeant suddenly look in the direction of the bushes at the side of the path.

We crossed the terrace, and went down the steps.

'A moment ago, I saw Rosanna Spearman hiding in the bushes,' said the Sergeant. 'Has she a lover? If she has, she may be waiting for him. If she hasn't, then her hiding looks highly suspicious.'

I knew that this was Mr Franklin's favourite walking place. Penelope had several times caught Rosanna hanging about here, as if waiting for him. I told the Sergeant that Rosanna might be in love with Mr Franklin.

We went back to the house. The Sergeant began questioning the servants one by one, in my room. Afterwards, he said that if Rosanna wanted permission to go out, I should let her go, but I should tell him about it straight away.

We were interrupted by a message from the cook. Rosanna had asked to go out, saying that her head was bad, and she wanted some fresh air. I said she could go.

'Lock the door of your room,' said the Sergeant, 'and if anybody asks for me, tell them I'm in there.' Then he disappeared.

Rosanna is a suspect

It was clear that, after he had spoken to the servants, something made Sergeant Cuff suspect Rosanna. I went to talk to them myself.

Two of the maids had not believed that Rosanna was really ill on the previous afternoon. They had knocked at her door, which was locked, and listened and not heard anyone moving around inside. They had seen a light under the door at midnight, and had heard the noise of a fire burning in the room at four o'clock in the morning.

I felt very sorry for Rosanna. Later, in the garden, I met Mr Franklin. I told him what I had heard from the two

maids. Mr Franklin thought Rosanna must have pretended to be ill in order to go to town for some guilty reason. He was sure the paint-stained dress was hers. She lit the fire to destroy it. Rosanna was the thief! He was about to
5 go and tell his aunt, when Sergeant Cuff appeared behind him.

'I will have no more to do with this case, if you say anything to anyone about it, before I give you permission,' he said sternly. Angrily, Mr Franklin agreed, and left us.
10 The Sergeant took my arm. He asked if there was a path leading to the beach from the house. I told him there was, and that I would show it to him. We set out for the Shivering Sand.

'Rosanna is being used'

15 As we walked along the path to the coast, Sergeant Cuff told me what he had been thinking about the case.

'Mr Betteredge,' said the Sergeant, 'first let me say that Rosanna is not the thief. She is being used by someone else. Now you heard yourself what the two maids noticed
20 when they went up to Rosanna's room. Here is what I think she was doing.

'On Thursday morning, Inspector Seegrave pointed out the mark on the door. Well, I think Rosanna found the paint on her dress, pretended to be ill, and went into
25 town. She bought the materials for a new dress, and made it on Thursday night. That explains why there was a light in her room so late. She kept the other dress hidden — she did not burn it — and at this moment I think she is on her way to hide it somewhere. I followed her earlier
30 this evening to a cottage in that fishing village on the coast.'

'Cobb's Hole,' I said. 'She is friendly with a family there — the Yollands.'

'Well, when she came out, she had something hidden
35 under her coat. I saw her set off along the coast. We may

be able to tell, by her footmarks in the sand, what she has been doing.'

By now it was getting dark. We looked out over the quicksand, which was shivering gently.

'I saw Rosanna walking in this direction,' said the Sergeant. 'Can we get to Cobb's Hole now that the tide is out? I would like to talk to the people she visited.'

'Yes, we can get there if we hurry,' I answered.

Sergeant Cuff suddenly bent down to look at the sand.

'A woman's footprints, Mr Betteredge!' he said. 'Look how she has tried to hide her tracks, for there is one footstep going to Cobb's Hole, and another coming from it. She probably walked through the water from this point until she got to those rocks, and came back the same way. Let us go on to the cottage.'

Rosanna had been friendly with the Yollands for some
time. Their daughter had a badly-shaped foot, and was
known as 'Limping Lucy'. Mrs Yolland asked us into her
kitchen. Sergeant Cuff told her he was making inquiries
about the loss of the Diamond. He said he was trying to
prove that Rosanna was innocent.

'I am afraid Rosanna Spearman will never be successful
in her present job after this,' said the Sergeant, sadly.

'Well, she will be leaving it soon anyway!' said Mrs
Yolland.

A letter to a friend

As the head servant at the house, I was very surprised to
hear this! The Sergeant did not seem surprised, however.
He asked if Rosanna had friends to go to.

'She has,' said Mrs Yolland. 'She came here this evening,
and asked to go to Lucy's room. "I want to write a letter
to a friend," she said. Who it was, I don't know.'

Mrs Yolland said that she had sold the girl some things
for her journey: an old tin case, and two dog chains to
tie round it.

As we walked back, the Sergeant continued to share
his thoughts with me. 'She won't use those things for
travelling,' he said. 'She has sunk the case in the water or
the quicksand, and fastened the chain to some place under
the rocks. When this trouble has died down, she will pull
the case up again. But what is in it? It's not the Diamond.'

'The marked dress!' I said.

'But why didn't she just throw the dress into the
Shivering Sand? Then it would have been gone for ever,'
said the Sergeant, puzzled.

When we got back outside the house, we learnt from
the policeman who had stayed to help Sergeant Cuff, that
Rosanna had returned nearly an hour ago. We also heard
that Miss Rachel had decided to leave, and my lady was
waiting to see the Sergeant.

Is Miss Rachel the thief?

When we went to see my lady, she told us that Miss Rachel was going to stay with her aunt, Mrs Ablewhite, in the morning.

'Can you stop her from going until later?' asked the Sergeant. 'I must go into Frizinghall tomorrow morning, and I shall be back about two o'clock. I want to speak to her.'

My lady asked me to tell the coachman that the carriage was not to come for Miss Rachel until two o'clock.

'You know something about Miss Rachel,' I said to the Sergeant when we were alone, 'and you've been hiding it from me all this time!'

'Ah,' said Sergeant Cuff, 'you've guessed it at last. Miss Verinder has had the Moonstone all the time. She has told Rosanna all about it because she thinks we will suspect her.'

I could not believe that Miss Rachel was guilty.

Some time later Samuel brought me a note from the local judge, saying that the Indians would shortly be set free. I gave this message to the Sergeant. He said he would visit Murthwaite in Frizinghall in the morning, and use him as his translator. There were some questions he wanted to ask the mysterious Indians.

I met Penelope in the passage. My daughter was as upset as I about the way things had changed in the house.

'I feel as if some dreadful misfortune is hanging over us all,' she said.

'He will not look at me!'

Just at that moment Rosanna ran past us. She looked very unhappy.

'For God's sake, don't speak to me,' she cried, when I asked her what was wrong.

A moment later Mr Franklin appeared in the hall with a look of amazement on his face.

'If that girl has something to do with the Diamond,' he said, 'I believe she was about to tell me. I was knocking the balls about on the billiard table, when she came in. I asked if she wanted to speak to me. She answered, "Yes, if I dare." I just went on knocking the balls about because I was feeling awkward. She suddenly turned away. "He looks at the billiard-balls," I heard her say. "But he will not look at me!" And then she left! Would you mind telling Rosanna that I did not mean to be unkind?'

As I checked the house that night before going to bed, I found Sergeant Cuff lying on three chairs placed right across the passage next to Miss Rachel's room. 'Why aren't you in your bed?' I asked.

'I am sure something happened this evening,' answered the Sergeant, 'between the time Rosanna returned from the Sand, and the time Miss Verinder said she was leaving. Whatever Rosanna hid in that box, it's clear to me that Miss Rachel couldn't go away until she knew that it was hidden. If the two of them try to get together, I want to be in the way, and stop them.'

But Rosanna did not try to see Miss Rachel that night.

Sergeant Cuff lays a trap

Early next morning Sergeant Cuff and I joined Mr Franklin on his favourite walk through the gardens. Sergeant Cuff was very anxious to know what Rosanna had said to Mr Franklin the night before, but the young man refused   5
to speak of it to him.

Suddenly, we saw Rosanna Spearman herself! She was followed by Penelope, who seemed to be trying to make her return to the house. When she saw that Mr Franklin was not alone, Rosanna stopped.   10

The Sergeant pretended not to have noticed the girls. Before either Mr Franklin or I could say a word, he said loudly, 'You needn't be afraid of harming the girl, sir. In fact, I would like to know if you have any interest in Rosanna Spearman.'   15

Mr Franklin, also pretending not to have noticed the girls, answered quickly, 'No, I have no interest at all in Rosanna Spearman.'

Rosanna turned round the moment Mr Franklin had spoken. She now let my daughter lead her back to the   20
house.

Sergeant Cuff then left to go to Frizinghall, saying he would be back before two.

'You must speak to Rosanna,' said Mr Franklin, when we were alone. 'I said what I did to stop her from saying   25
anything in front of Sergeant Cuff. He was obviously trying to trap me into talking about her. I didn't want to do anything to help him.'

The hours passed slowly. Miss Rachel stayed in her room. Mr Franklin went for a long walk alone.   30

Penelope came to see me privately. She said that Mr Franklin's words that morning had hurt Rosanna cruelly.

'Why was Rosanna out there this morning?' I asked.

'She was determined to speak to Mr Franklin,' said   35
Penelope. 'I tried to stop her. If I could only have got her

away before she heard Mr Franklin say what he did. I
know he did it in her best interests. But those words
turned her to stone. She has gone about ever since in a
dream.'

Rosanna has something on her mind

I had promised Mr Franklin I would speak to Rosanna,
and this seemed to be the right time. We found the girl
sweeping the passage by the bedrooms and I tried to
explain what had happened, as best I could.

'Mr Franklin is very kind. Please thank him,' she
answered.

I saw that she was speaking as if in a dream. She went
on sweeping all the time. As gently as I could, I made her
stop work and listen to me.

'Come, come, my girl,' I said. 'This isn't like you. You
have got something on your mind. I shall still be your
friend, even if you have done something wrong. Can't you
talk about it?'

She said she could, but she would only talk to
Mr Franklin.

I thought we ought to get a doctor for the girl, but
Mr Candy was still ill, and I did not like to call his assistant,
Ezra Jennings. Nobody knew much about him, and none
of us liked him. There were other doctors, but Penelope
thought it might do more harm than good to bring in
someone that none of us knew.

A TERRIBLE DEATH

Miss Rachel leaves

I wanted to tell my lady of the peculiar way in which Rosanna was behaving, but she was with Miss Rachel. I waited until the clock struck quarter to two. Five minutes afterwards, I met Sergeant Cuff returning from Frizinghall. 5

'I have seen the Indians,' he said. 'They have no more to do with the loss of the jewel than you have. But I can tell you, Mr Betteredge, if we don't find it, they will.'

'What about Rosanna?' I asked.

'I have found the shop she went to,' he said. 'She 10 bought a piece of plain cotton material, enough to make a nightgown. Between the hours of twelve and three, on Thursday morning, she must have crept down to Miss Rachel's room, brushing against the wet paint on the door. She couldn't destroy the nightgown without first making 15 another, or the list of her clothes would show that something was missing.'

'What makes you think it was her nightgown?' I asked.

'The material she bought,' answered the Sergeant. 'If it had been Miss Verinder's nightgown, she would have had 20 to buy better material and some ribbons and lace. She wouldn't have had time to make it in one night. The question is, why did she hide the one with the paint on instead of destroying it? That hiding-place at the Shivering Sand must be searched.' 25

Then the carriage came to take Miss Rachel to her aunt's. No more than a minute later, Miss Rachel ran downstairs. She kissed her mother in a hurry.

'Try to forgive me, Mamma,' she said as she ran to the carriage. Sergeant Cuff held the carriage door open. 30

'I want to say, Miss, that your leaving us as things are now, makes it difficult for me to find your Diamond.'

Miss Rachel never even answered him. 'Drive on, James!' she called out to the coachman.

The Sergeant shut the carriage door. Just as he closed it, Mr Franklin came running down the steps.

5 'Goodbye, Rachel,' he said, holding out his hand.

'Drive on!' cried Miss Rachel, taking no more notice of him than she had of the Sergeant.

Mr Franklin stepped back 10 as if he had been struck in the face. The coach pulled away.

'Betteredge,' said Mr Franklin, turning to me with tears in his eyes, 'get me away to the train as soon as you can!' He and my lady went back into the house.

15 Sergeant Cuff and I were left at the bottom of the steps.

'Your young lady has got a travelling companion in the carriage with her,' he remarked, 'and the name of it is the Moonstone.'

I said nothing. I only held on to my belief in Miss 20 Rachel.

Rosanna is missing

Soon after Miss Rachel left the house, it was discovered that Rosanna Spearman was missing. The last person to have seen her was Nancy, the kitchen-maid.

Nancy had seen her slip out with a letter in her hand, and had heard her ask the butcher's man to post it from Frizinghall. The man had looked at the address, and had said it was a round-about way of delivering a letter to Cobb's Hole. However, he had promised to post it, and had driven away. No one else had seen Rosanna Spearman after that.

'Well,' said the Sergeant, 'I must go to Frizinghall. I am sure a note about the hiding-place will be in that letter. I must see it at the post office. If it is what I suspect, I shall pay Mrs Yolland another visit.'

Before he could set off, one of the garden boys, known as 'Duffy', ran up and said that he had seen Rosanna half an hour ago, in the fir wood, going in the direction of the seashore.

Sergeant Cuff and Duffy started out for the Shivering Sand quickly. Some time after, Duffy came running back with a note from the Sergeant asking for one of Rosanna Spearman's boots.

I sent for one, and took it as quickly as I could.

As I got near the shore, I heard the thunder of the sea on the sandbank at the mouth of the bay. Then I saw the great rough waves rolling in, and the black figure of Sergeant Cuff standing on the beach.

The Shivering Sand

I went down to him, and I saw in his eyes a look of horror. He took the boot from me and set it in a footprint. It fitted exactly. The footprint pointed towards the rocky ledge called the South Spit. Sergeant Cuff followed the footsteps down to where the rocks and sand joined. There was no sign of any footsteps walking away from the rocks.

In silence he looked at me. I knew what he was thinking. A dreadful trembling crept over me.

'Some serious accident has happened on those rocks,' Sergeant Cuff said.

I remembered how she had been in the passage. I remembered her again as I had seen her when she was late for dinner and I had gone to find her. I heard her telling me that the Shivering Sand seemed to draw her to
5 it against her will, and that her grave was waiting for her there.

From the sand-hills, the men-servants from the house and the fisherman, Yolland, came running down to us. They called out to ask if the girl had been found.

10 The Sergeant silently pointed to the footprints. He turned to Yolland and asked, 'Is there any chance of finding her, when the tide goes out?'

'None,' was the answer. 'What the Sand gets, the Sand keeps for ever.'

15 Sergeant Cuff went on to say that in his opinion, Rosanna had not slipped off the Spit by accident. There was a shelf of rock three feet under the Sand, which would have saved her. She must have made up her mind to walk into the deep Sand beyond the ledge.

20 We had turned back towards the house, when a man-servant came running to give me a note. It had been written by Rosanna. In it she said that she had found her grave where it was waiting for her. She asked for my forgiveness.

25 Silently we went back to the house.

We found the servants and my lady horrified at what had happened. Penelope told Sergeant Cuff that Rosanna had killed herself for love of Mr Franklin, but I said I was certain that Mr Franklin knew nothing of the poor girl's
30 feelings. We agreed not to tell him about Rosanna's feelings. Her death was not his fault.

A bold experiment

Half an hour later, I met Mr Franklin coming out of his aunt's sitting-room. He said that her ladyship was ready
35 to see Sergeant Cuff, and would like me to be there.

Sergeant Cuff asked Mr Franklin if he would like to come with us to speak to Lady Verinder. He answered no. He added in a whisper to me, 'I know what the man is going to say about Rachel. I don't want to hear it.'

I knew how he felt. Sergeant Cuff and I went together.

'I believe that Rosanna Spearman killed herself because she knew something,' began the Sergeant. 'Something so terrible that it forced her to take her own life. But the only person who can tell me whether I am right or wrong has left this house.'

'You mean my daughter,' said my lady. 'You suspect Miss Verinder of deceiving us all by hiding the Diamond for some reason of her own. I can tell you, that she could not possibly have done this. I know my child.'

She faced the Sergeant steadily. Sergeant Cuff bowed.

'I know that young ladies sometimes have private debts, which they dare not talk about, even to their relatives,' he said. 'Miss Verinder has refused to be questioned, and was very rude to Chief Inspector Seegrave, myself, and young Mr Franklin. Why should she be offended by the three people who have all been trying to get back her valuable stolen Diamond? My own experience in these matters suggests that she has debts to be paid, and has been forced to sell the Diamond secretly, to pay them. If Miss Verinder does not know where the jewel is, why is she behaving in such a way?

'When Rosanna Spearman was a thief, she knew people who would buy good jewellery and not ask questions. I think she and Miss Rachel were working together. In order to end this inquiry, I am going to try a bold experiment. I want to tell Miss Verinder, without any warning, of Rosanna's death. She may be so upset that she will tell us the truth. Does your ladyship agree?'

'Yes, but I shall put her to the test myself. You will stay here, and I will go to Frizinghall. And I will let you know the result of the experiment before the last train leaves for London tonight.'

With that, she called for a carriage, and drove off to Frizinghall.

The inquiry is ended

The carriage returned with two letters, one for Mr Franklin,
5   and the other for me. Inside my letter was a cheque made out to Sergeant Cuff, to pay him for the work he had done. I read the letter to him.

'My good Gabriel, Miss Verinder declares that she has never spoken a word in private to Rosanna. She swears
10 that she doesn't owe anyone any money, and that the Diamond has never been in her possession since she put it into her cabinet on Wednesday. She remains silent when I ask if she can explain its disappearance. All she will say is, "The day will come when you will know why I don't
15 care about being suspected, and why I am silent, even to you. I have done nothing which you would be ashamed of." Read my letter to Sergeant Cuff, and give him the money. I do not wish him to continue the inquiry any more.'

20 The Sergeant nodded.

'Before I go,' he said, 'I'll tell you three things which will happen in the future. You will hear something from the Yollands when the postman delivers Rosanna's letter at Cobb's Hole. You will hear of the three Indians, in
25 Frizinghall if Miss Rachel stays there, or in London if Miss Rachel goes to London. Third, you will hear of Septimus Luker of London, money-lender and buyer of stolen property. Rosanna Spearman used to know him. Time will tell whether I'm right or not. Goodbye, sir.' He shook my
30 hand, and left the house.

Mr Franklin left us by the train that night. The letter sent by his aunt had said that Rachel, still in a very nervous state, remained silent about the loss of her jewel. She continued to blame Mr Franklin for having tried to uncover
35 the mystery. Her ladyship intended taking her to London,

to give her a complete change, and also to see a doctor. I was very sorry for Mr Franklin. I knew how fond of Miss Rachel he was. I felt that the Moonstone had certainly helped the Colonel to get his revenge.

Limping Lucy

On the next day, Sunday, my mistress sent me a message to say that she was now taking Rachel to London. Most of the other servants were to follow. I was to stay in the country to look after things.

On the Monday, the first of the things that Sergeant Cuff had said would happen came true.

I was walking in the garden, not far from the house, when I came across the fisherman's daughter, Limping Lucy, who demanded fiercely to see Mr Franklin. I asked her what she wanted with him, and she said she had a letter to give him from Rosanna!

'Mr Franklin went to London last night,' I said, 'but I'll send the letter on to him by post.'

'No, I am to give it to him myself,' said Lucy. 'If he wants the letter, he must come and get it from me.'

And she limped off home to Cobb's Hole.

On Tuesday morning I received two letters. One said that my lady and Miss Rachel had arrived in London. The other informed me that Mr Franklin Blake had left England to travel abroad.

This news put an end to my hopes of bringing Limping Lucy and Mr Franklin together. Whether Rosanna had killed herself for love of Mr Franklin, and the letter contained the confession she was about to make to him while she was alive, it was impossible to say.

On Thursday I had a letter from Penelope, in London, telling me the latest news. Miss Rachel's doctor said that she needed to get out and enjoy herself, so several parties had been arranged. Mr Godfrey had called. Penelope, who did not like him, was sorry to see him welcomed in a very friendly manner. My mistress was not very well, and had seen her lawyer twice. Miss Clack, a distant relative who had been one of the guests at the dinner, was always calling at the house. She was becoming a great nuisance by always trying to help when her help was not needed.

On Saturday a London newspaper arrived from Sergeant Cuff. He had marked a police report, which read:

LAMBETH— Mr Septimus Luker stated that he had been annoyed throughout the day by three Indians. Mr Luker was worried in case they intended to rob him. The day before, he had dismissed a man from his employment on suspicion of theft. He felt that this man and the three Indians might be working together.

So Sergeant Cuff had been right. All that he had said would happen had happened, in less than a week. After hearing from the Yollands on the Monday, I had now heard of the Indians, and heard of the money-lender in the news from London — Miss Rachel herself being also in London.

Here then, is the end of my part in this mystery. The story of the Diamond continues in London.

Part 2
The Discovery of the Truth (1848–1849)

**The first story, told by Miss Drusilla Clack,
niece of the late Sir John Verinder**

THE ENGAGEMENT

Mr Godfrey Ablewhite is attacked

I have been asked by Mr Franklin Blake to help him in
writing the story of the Moonstone. I will tell of the events
which took place while I was visiting my Aunt Verinder's
house in London.

On Monday 3rd July 1848, I discovered that my aunt
and her daughter were in London. I immediately went to
their house and sent up a message asking if I could be of
any help to them. My aunt replied with an invitation to
lunch the next day.

That evening I went to a meeting of a Charity Society
committee. My cousin, Mr Godfrey Ablewhite, was also a
member of this committee, and I expected to see him
there. To our great disappointment he never came. We
ladies of the Charity Society committee greatly admire
Mr Godfrey Ablewhite. His understanding of the world
and his excellent business sense help us so much. He is
our leader in the good work we do. One of the other
members told me what had happened to him.

On the previous Friday, she said, Mr Godfrey was at a
bank in Lombard Street. As he was leaving, another man,
a complete stranger, left at exactly the same moment. Each
man stood back to allow the other to pass through the
doorway first. They exchanged a few polite words, and
then parted.

When Mr Godfrey arrived home, he found a boy waiting to give him a letter. He was asked to go to a house in Northumberland Street to see an elderly lady who wished to give a large sum of money to charity.

5   Mr Godfrey went at once. When he arrived, he was shown into an empty room at the back of the house. He was seized round the neck from behind. He had just time to notice that the arm holding onto him was dark brown, before his eyes and mouth were covered, and he was

10 thrown to the floor by two men. A third man went through his pockets. Some words were spoken in a foreign language. He was bound hand and foot, and left there.

Mr Godfrey was rescued soon afterwards by some other people who lived in the house. They had seen three

15 foreign gentlemen leaving in a hurry, and felt suspicious. Mr Godfrey's property was scattered all over the floor, but nothing seemed to be missing.

The man who had left the bank at the same time as Mr Godfrey had had a similar unfortunate experience. In

20 his case, one of the papers he had been carrying had been taken. It was a receipt for something valuable which he had left at his bank. The paper was of no use to anyone, because only the owner could collect the valuable from the bank. The name of this man was Mr Septimus Luker.

25 The thieves had obviously seen Mr Godfrey speaking to Mr Luker at the bank, and thought that something had been given to him.

Rachel questions Mr Godfrey

On Tuesday, I went to see Aunt Verinder. She told me the

30 whole awful story of the Moonstone. Later Mr Godfrey Ablewhite walked in. He said he did not want to talk about his unfortunate adventure, but cousin Rachel was determined to question him!

'People are saying, aren't they, that these three men are

35 the three Indians who came to our house in the country?

And Mr Luker was robbed of a receipt which he had got from his bankers, wasn't he? What was the receipt for?'

'For a valuable stone, I believe,' said Mr Godfrey.

'People are also saying that Mr Luker's valuable stone is the Moonstone,' continued Rachel.

'Mr Luker has declared that he had never heard of the Moonstone,' Mr Godfrey replied.

'And has anyone said anything about you, Godfrey?

Mr Godfrey looked very uncomfortable. 'Most people are saying that I took the Moonstone to Mr Luker and asked him to lend me some money,' he answered.

Rachel jumped to her feet.

'This is my fault! I must put it right. I may make my own life unhappy if I so wish it, but I cannot let an innocent man be ruined! Mamma! Miss Clack! I know that Godfrey Ablewhite is innocent. Write a declaration of your innocence, Godfrey, and I will sign it.'

Mr Godfrey wrote out the declaration. She signed it, and gave it back to him, asking him to show it everywhere. Then some of her friends arrived, and she left us to visit a flower show.

When Rachel had gone, Mr Godfrey came over to us, with his declaration and a box of matches in his hands.

'Dear aunt,' he said, 'please say nothing to Rachel. Let her think that I accept her self-sacrifice. And now, will you witness that I destroy it?'

He lit the paper and let it burn away. Then he left us.

Lady Verinder's illness

Lady Verinder then turned to me. 'Drusilla,' she said, 'I have been seriously ill for some months. No doctor can help me. I am suffering from a heart disease. I may die
5 before one more day has passed. I have told this only to my sister, to Mr Bruff, who is my lawyer, and now to you. I don't want Rachel to know about it. I have written my will, and Mr Bruff will bring it here this afternoon for my signature. I would like you to be here too, as a witness.'
10   I was so pleased that my aunt had asked me to help her. In my possession were many good Christian books which I knew would prepare her for her last hours. I had just time to hurry home to get some. I returned before five o'clock for the witnessing of the will.
15   When I arrived, the doctor was with Lady Verinder. Mr Bruff was waiting in the library. I was shown into the library too.

'Well, Miss Clack,' said Mr Bruff, 'How is your good friend, Mr Godfrey Ablewhite? I've recently heard a very
20 interesting story about him!'

'I have heard it,' I answered, 'and I know it is a lie.'

'Ah, Miss Clack. Mr Godfrey Ablewhite won't find many people so willing to believe him as you charitable ladies. He was in the house when the Diamond was lost, and
25 the first person in the house to go to London afterwards. It looks bad for him.'

'Let me tell you, Mr Bruff,' I said, 'that Mr Godfrey was in this house a short while ago, and Miss Verinder herself swore that he was innocent.'

30   Mr Bruff looked very surprised at this news.

'If Rachel says that he is innocent, Miss Clack, then I believe it,' he said when I told him what had happened. 'From now on, whenever I hear of that story, I will say that it is not true.'

35   He turned away from me and began walking up and down.

'You mentioned, sir,' I said, 'that Mr Godfrey was in the house at the time the Diamond was lost. Mr Franklin Blake was also in the house at that time, and his debts are well known.'

Mr Bruff looked at me.

'Most of the people Franklin Blake owes money to are quite happy to wait for their money, Miss Clack. They know his father is a very rich man. Also, Lady Verinder has told me that her daughter was ready to marry Franklin Blake before the Diamond disappeared from the house, and that he knew this. So why should he steal the Moonstone? No, Miss Clack! There is no doubt of Rachel's innocence, nor, now, of Mr Ablewhite's innocence, nor of Franklin Blake's either. And yet somebody brought the Moonstone to London, because I am sure that Mr Luker, or his banker, is in possession of it at this moment.'

At this point a servant came in to say that my aunt was waiting to see us. We went in silence to Lady Verinder's room.

Good Christian books

The signing of the will did not take long. As soon as we were alone, my aunt lay back on the sofa.

'I hope you won't think that I have forgotten you in my will, Drusilla,' she said. 'I will give you a little gift before I die.'

Here was the opportunity I had been waiting for! I opened my bag, and took out the top book. It was about the Evil One, and how to avoid him.

'Read this, dear aunt, and you will have done enough for me,' I said.

Lady Verinder glanced at the book and handed it back to me, saying that the doctor had ordered that she read only amusing books. I said that I would leave it for her to read when she felt stronger, and left her to sleep. I placed one or two more in other rooms around the house,

ending with my aunt's bedroom and bathroom. Then I left
the house.

The next morning, just as I was getting ready to go to
see my aunt, Samuel called with a parcel under his arm.

'From my lady, Miss.'

I asked him if my aunt was at home. No, he said, she
had gone out for a drive. Miss Rachel and Mr Ablewhite
had gone too. Knowing how much charitable work
Mr Godfrey had to do, I thought it odd that he should be
wasting time on a drive. I made a few more inquiries.
Miss Rachel was going to a dance that night with
Mr Ablewhite, and they were going to a concert the
following day!

When I was alone, I opened the parcel to find my
precious books, all returned 'by the doctor's orders'! I
decided to pay another visit to the house.

Soon after two o'clock, I knocked at my aunt's front
door. Lady Verinder was resting. I said I would wait in the
library.

The house was quiet, so I thought Rachel must have
already gone to the concert. Then I heard a knock at the
street door. The next moment I heard a man's footsteps
approaching. I thought it must be the doctor. I did not
want to meet him. He had insulted me by telling my aunt
to return my books, so I went into the drawing room and
hid behind the curtains.

I was greatly surprised when the visitor came into the
drawing room. I heard him walking restlessly backwards
and forwards, talking to himself. It was Mr Godfrey's voice!
And the words I heard him speak were, 'I'll do it today!'

'Please be my wife!'

Suddenly I heard another voice in the room: Rachel
Verinder's.

'Why have you come up here, Godfrey?' she said. 'Why
didn't you go into the library?'

He answered, 'Miss Clack is there.'

To show myself now was impossible. I noiselessly arranged the curtains so that I could both see and hear.

Mr Godfrey sat next to Rachel, looking at her. Then he drew close and took her hand.

'Rachel, am I mad to dream of a day when you may become more to me than just a friend?'

'Are you really so fond of me? At this moment I am the unhappiest girl alive. I hate myself!'

'My dear Rachel! Don't speak like this! Your behaviour concerning the Moonstone may seem strange — '

'I'm not talking about the Moonstone. If the true story of the Moonstone is ever told, it will be known that I was keeping a horrible secret. Godfrey, I am in love with someone whom I found does not deserve it. And I can't put him out of my heart. He doesn't know and I will never see him again! Don't ask me his name! Don't pity me! For God's sake, go away!'

Mr Godfrey fell on his knees at her feet.

'Rachel,' he said, 'please be my wife! I don't ask for your love. I will be content with your fondness, and…'

'Godfrey,' she answered, 'you must be mad. If I say yes, we may both be sorry when it's too late. You ask me for more than I can give.'

But Mr Godfrey would not be refused. 'My dearest,' he said, 'I only ask you to give me yourself.' He drew her nearer to him until her face touched his.

I could see that Rachel was unable to help herself. Mr Godfrey is a very persuasive speaker. When he decides he wants something, he usually gets his way. At last Rachel agreed. 'We shall say nothing to my mother about this until she is better,' she said. 'I wish it to be kept a secret for the present. Go now, and come back this evening.'

She rose, and looked at the curtains where I was hiding. 'Who has done that?' she said. 'It's hot enough in here without keeping the air out like that.'

She came towards the curtains, as if to open them. But at that moment, the voice of the footman, stopped her.

'Miss Rachel!' he called out. 'My lady has fainted, and nothing we do seems to help her.'

In a moment more I was alone, and free to go downstairs without being seen.

Mr Godfrey passed me in the hall, hurrying out to fetch the doctor. 'Go in and help them,' he said, pointing to the room.

I found Rachel on her knees by the sofa. Lady Verinder was dead. My aunt had died without reading my books. She had also died without leaving me my little gift.

Mr Bruff comes to visit

A month went by before I saw Rachel Verinder again. After Lady Verinder's death, Mr Ablewhite — Mr Godfrey's father, who was Lady Verinder's brother-in-law — was named as Rachel's guardian. The family now knew of Rachel's engagement to Mr Godfrey.

It was arranged that Mr Ablewhite would rent a house in Brighton for his wife and Rachel. Godfrey would travel backwards and forwards between London and Brighton. Rachel asked me to stay with her, as her guest, and my Aunt Ablewhite asked me to hire some servants and get the house ready.

In a few days all the arrangements had been made. I thought Rachel would be a better person if she read some

of my Christian books, so placed a few in the rooms she
would be likely to use. On the Saturday afternoon, I
waited for my relatives to arrive.

To my surprise, the lawyer, Mr Bruff, came with them.
Mr Godfrey had not been able to come, and Mr Bruff had   5
taken his place.

I felt sure that Mr Bruff had some special reason for
coming to Brighton. Through dinner I saw him looking at
Rachel with great interest.

The next day at lunch, Rachel said she had a headache.   10
Mr Bruff suggested a walk, and they went off together. He
must have said what he wanted to say then. When Rachel
returned, she was unusually silent and thoughtful, and did
not come down for dinner. Mr Bruff left early, to return
to London next day.   15

Next morning I took her tea to her. I noticed my precious
books on a table in a corner of her room. She told me
that they had not interested her. However, I forgave her
for being so rude, and I asked her gently whether Mr Bruff
had given her some bad news the day before.   20

'Not at all!' she exclaimed fiercely. 'I'm very grateful to
Mr Bruff for telling me what he did. Drusilla, I shall never
marry Mr Godfrey Ablewhite.'

'But everything is settled!' I cried.

'Wait until Godfrey arrives here today,' she said, 'and   25
you will see that I am right.'

The engagement is ended

I went for a walk for the rest of the morning, having first
discovered the time when Mr Godfrey was to arrive. At
about that time, I went back to the house. I entered the   30
dining room — and found myself alone with him!

He told me he had already seen Rachel. She had broken
their engagement. And what's more, he had allowed her
to break it! I was so surprised at this news that I had to
sit down.   35

Mr Godfrey sat down next to me.

'I don't know why I asked Miss Verinder to marry me,' he sighed. 'Works of charity are what give me the most happiness in life. She loves another man. I am rather relieved that it is all over.'

He looked at the clock.

'I'll have to hurry, or I'll miss the train,' he exclaimed. 'My father is coming here tomorrow. I must meet him in London and tell him what has happened. He will be disappointed. He wanted this marriage very much. Well, he must get used to the idea that it will not take place. Goodbye, my friend.'

He hurried out, and I ran upstairs to my own room.

The next day Mr Ablewhite, Mr Godfrey's father, arrived, followed by Mr Bruff. Old Mr Ablewhite was very angry. He thought Rachel's change of heart about Mr Godfrey was an insult to him. I tried my best to keep everyone calm. I remembered some excellent words in one of my Christian books, and asked if I could read them out. Unfortunately, this only made Mr Ablewhite even angrier.

'Who asked this mad woman into the house?' he shouted.

'Miss Clack is here as my guest,' said Rachel.

These words suddenly changed Mr Ablewhite. From his state of red-hot anger, he became cold and distant.

'Oh?' he said. 'Miss Clack is here as your guest in my house?'

'Mr Ablewhite,' interrupted Mr Bruff, 'you took this house, as Miss Verinder's guardian, for her use.'

'If my son is not good enough to be Miss Verinder's husband,' said Mr Ablewhite, 'I am not good enough to be Miss Verinder's guardian. I beg Miss Verinder to remove her guest and her luggage, as soon as possible.' He made a low bow and walked out of the room.

As soon as the door closed, Aunt Ablewhite crossed the room.

'My dear,' she said, taking Rachel's hand, 'let me apologize for the way in which my husband has spoken to you.' Then she looked at me, angrily. 'Drusilla, be quiet,' she said. 'You made Mr Ablewhite lose his temper. I hope I shall never see you or your books again.'

I forgave her rudeness like a true Christian.

Aunt Ablewhite left the room, and Mr Bruff led Rachel to a chair.

'My dear young lady,' he said, 'your mother's will gives me the right to advise the executors about a new guardian. Will you honour me by coming to stay as my guest until the business is decided?'

My heart rose when I heard that there would be a new guardian. Rachel was like a younger sister to me. With my guidance, and the help of my books, I knew Rachel could be much improved. However, before I could interrupt, Rachel had accepted Mr Bruff's invitation.

'Stop!' I said. 'I ask the executors to appoint me guardian.'

Rachel looked at me with cruel dislike.

'I think it will be best if I remain under Mr Bruff's care,' she said.

She and Mr Bruff went out of the room, leaving me alone.

7

THE INDIAN PLOT

Lady Verinder's will

There are two reasons for my being asked to write next. First, I knew the true story of the broken engagement between Godfrey Ablewhite and Miss Rachel. Second, I
5   found myself part of the mystery of the Diamond.

To begin with the engagement.

The late Sir John Verinder, when he died, left all his property to his wife. Shortly afterwards, Lady Verinder sent for me, and made her first will. Her daughter was well
10 provided for.

The will remained at my office till the summer of 1848. When Lady Verinder knew that she had not long to live, she decided to make a few changes, and I advised her to make a second will, which she did.

15 About three weeks after Lady Verinder's death, I found out that Mr Smalley, another lawyer, had asked to see her will. I went to find out why he wanted it. Mr Smalley said that one of his clients wanted to know about the will. The client, I learnt, was Mr Godfrey
20 Ablewhite.

I didn't need to hear any more.

Lady Verinder had been afraid that someone might want to marry Rachel just for her money. So she had done something to prevent this. According to the new will,
25 Rachel and her husband would have a house in London and one in Yorkshire. They could live in these houses,

but they were not allowed to sell them. They would also have a yearly income to use as they wished, but they were not allowed to sell any of the shares or property that produced the income.

Godfrey had asked to see Lady Verinder's will. If he was only interested in money, would he still want to marry Rachel, after what he had discovered? If he did not need a large amount of money at once, then it would still be worth marrying Rachel for her income alone. However, if he needed a great deal of money immediately, Lady Verinder's will would save her daughter from making a serious mistake.

I went to Brighton, as Miss Clack has said, and told Rachel my fears soon after I arrived. She didn't say a word until I had finished. Then she looked at me with a smile.

'Thank you so much for telling me this,' she said. 'My marriage will no longer take place.'

When I heard that she had decided to break her engagement, I advised her to tell Godfrey that she had proof that he was only interested in her money. If he said it wasn't true, she was to send him to me.

'Mr Bruff, I cannot be so cruel to my cousin,' she answered. 'The only explanation I shall give is that I have thought it over, and that I am satisfied it will be best for both of us if we part. No more than that.'

I went back to London feeling uneasy. I was not sure that Godfrey would agree with Rachel's explanation.

On the evening of my return, I was surprised by a visit from Mr Ablewhite, Godfrey's father. He told me that Mr Godfrey had been refused by Miss Verinder and that Mr Godfrey had accepted the refusal. It was obvious to me why Godfrey had given in so easily. He needed a lot of money quickly, and marrying Rachel would be of no help to him.

Miss Verinder stayed with my wife and myself until a new guardian was appointed. Then she left us.

A strange visitor

Shortly afterwards, I was informed at my office that
someone had called and presented his card. The words
'Mr Septimus Luker asks you to see this gentleman' were
5 written on it. My clerk said he thought the stranger was
Indian. I remembered the Moonstone, and at once decided
to see him.

The moment my mysterious client was shown in, I felt
that I was in the presence of one of the three Indians.
10 After first apologizing for disturbing me, he took out a
small parcel, wrapped in a golden cloth. Out of this, he
took a black wooden box covered in jewels. He asked me
to lend him some money, saying he would leave the box
as a promise that the money would be paid back. He had
15 been to see Mr Luker first, but Mr Luker had told him that
he had no money to lend, and sent him to me.

'I am sorry,' I said, 'but Mr Luker was wrong to send
you here. I never lend money to strangers.'

The Indian wrapped up his box again, and rose to go.
20 He did not seem very disappointed that I could not help
him.

'May I ask one question?' he said. 'Suppose you had
lent me the money, when would you have wanted me to
pay it back?'

25 'When people borrow money in this way, they are
usually expected to pay the money back in one year's
time,' I said. He looked straight at me as I answered his
question. Then he walked softly out of the room.

It was clear that he had not come to borrow money at
30 all, but to ask me that question.

After he had gone, a letter was brought to me from
Mr Septimus Luker, asking to see me. He came to my
office the following day. He told me that two days before,
the Indian had visited him. He had at once recognized
35 him as the chief of the three Indians who had annoyed
him by waiting around his house. He thought, too, that

this man was one of the Indians who had robbed him. He was very frightened.

The Indian had asked him for money, and Mr Luker had said that he had no money to lend. The Indian had then asked who was the best person to apply to for a loan. Mr Luker had given my name because I was the first person he could think of.

Before Mr Luker left me, I asked him if the Indian had said anything as he was leaving his house.

Yes! The Indian had asked exactly the same question that he had asked me, and Mr Luker had given him the same answer.

Mr Murthwaite explains the plot

I went out to dinner that evening, and found myself sitting next to none other than Mr Murthwaite. I knew that he had been at Lady Verinder's house the night before the Moonstone was lost, and that he had helped to question the Indians. I told him of the strange visitor that had come to see Mr Luker and myself the day before, and of his mysterious question.

'Why should he be so anxious to know the time at which someone who borrows money is likely to pay it back?' I asked Mr Murthwaite.

Mr Murthwaite explained the plot to me.

'The Indians' first chance of stealing the Diamond was offered to them by Colonel Herncastle's death. Up to that time, the Diamond was kept in the strong-room at the bank. The Colonel's will left it to his niece. They could easily apply to see the will, and it would tell them that the Moonstone was to be given to the daughter of Lady Verinder, and that Mr Blake was to take it to her. That is why they appeared at Frizinghall disguised as magicians. They knew that Franklin Blake had been to the bank, and was going to visit Lady Verinder.

'Franklin Blake had seen one of the spies in the street, so he changed the time of his arrival in Yorkshire by some hours. He had therefore taken the Diamond to the bank at Frizinghall before the Indians expected him in the neighbourhood.

'When the Indians found out what Mr Blake had done, they didn't go near the house for some weeks. They knew that the Moonstone was to be given to Miss Verinder on her birthday. They would wait until the Diamond was in her possession before trying again.

'They came to the house on Miss Verinder's birthday, and saw her wearing the Moonstone. However, the next day, when the Moonstone was lost, the three Indians were arrested and had no chance of continuing with their plans.

'A day or two before the Indians were set free, the governor of the prison came to me with a letter which had been sent to them. It was written in Hindustani. He wanted me to translate it. Here is what the letter said.'

He handed me his note-book. I read these words:

In the name of the Ruler of the Night, whose seat is on the Antelope, whose arms point to the four corners of the earth.

Brothers, turn your faces to the south, and come to me in the street of many noises, which leads down to the muddy river.

The reason is this. My own eyes have seen it.

'The god of the moon,' Mr Murthwaite explained, 'has four arms, and rides on an antelope.

One of his names is "the Ruler of the Night". This, then, must be about the Moonstone.

'The Indians were given their letter. On the day they were set free, they caught the first train to London. The next news we heard of them was that they were waiting around Mr Luker's house.

'Mr Luker had recently dismissed a foreign workman because he suspected he was a thief. This man and the three Indians were working together. I believe it was the workman who wrote that letter.

'Somebody must have taken the Moonstone from Yorkshire to London, and exchanged it for money. That was how it came into Mr Luker's possession. Mr Luker took the Diamond to the bank before the Indians could think of a plan for robbing him. The Moonstone is once more out of their reach.

'Their third chance of stealing the stone will come a year after the Moonstone was put into the bank. If the person who has borrowed the money can pay it back, then he will get the Diamond back at the end of June. The reason, therefore, for your Indian's mysterious question, was to find out when the Diamond will be taken from the bank.

'Whoever leaves that bank with the Moonstone in his pocket is in terrible danger. The Indians have lost two chances of taking it, Mr Bruff. I don't believe that they will lose again.'

I made a note of the date:

June, 1849. Expect news of the Indians, end of the month.

8

THE NIGHTGOWN

Back to Yorkshire

In the spring of the year 1849, when I was travelling in the East, I received a letter from my lawyer, Mr Bruff, telling me that my father was dead. My father was a very
5 rich man, and I was to receive almost all of his great fortune.

When I got to London, Mr Bruff told me everything that had happened while I was away.

I was pleased to hear that Rachel had broken off her
10 engagement to Godfrey Ablewhite. She was living with Mrs Merridew, her father's sister, in Portland Place. Half an hour later, I was on my way to see her!

The servant took my card upstairs. He came down again, and said that Miss Verinder was out. I said I would
15 call again, at six o'clock. At six o'clock I was told for the second time that Miss Verinder was not at home. It was clear that Rachel did not want to see me.

My servant took a letter to Rachel next day, and the answer came back in one sentence.

20 'Miss Verinder does not wish to write to Mr Franklin Blake.'

I saw Mr Bruff, but he could not help me. He said Rachel had never mentioned me while she was staying with him.

25 'I am going to Yorkshire by the next train,' I said. 'I am determined to find out what it is she seems to know about the theft of the Moonstone. I shall start the inquiry again, and my first questions will be to Gabriel Betteredge.'

That evening I arrived at my late aunt's house in
30 Yorkshire.

'Mr Franklin!' cried Betteredge when he opened the door. 'Come in, sir! Let me take your bags to your room.'

However, the house was now Rachel's and, after what had happened, I could not bring myself to stay there. I explained this to Betteredge. He looked disappointed, but said that there were rooms for visitors at a farmhouse only two miles away. We set off together for that place.

On the way I told him that I had returned to find out who took the Diamond. Betteredge shook his head.

'Leave the Diamond alone, Mr Franklin! It has done harm to everybody who has come near it.'

'Betteredge,' I replied, 'I know the Diamond is the cause of the way Rachel is treating me. My only chance is to look further into the mystery of the lost Moonstone.'

'Aren't you afraid of what you may find out about Miss Rachel?' asked Betteredge.

'I am as certain of her innocence as you are,' I said.

'Mr Franklin,' said Betteredge, 'I believe I can help you start your inquiries. Rosanna Spearman left an unopened letter behind her, addressed to you. Limping Lucy, the fisherman's daughter, at Cobb's Hole has it. She wouldn't give it to anyone but you. And you had left England before I could write to you.'

'Let's go back, Betteredge, and get it at once.'

'It's too late, sir, tonight. Come to the house tomorrow morning, and we'll go together to the fisherman's cottage.'

Rosanna's instructions

The next morning, impatient to get the letter, I set out without stopping for breakfast. I found Betteredge ready waiting for me.

The fisherman's wife was in her kitchen when we arrived at the cottage. She asked us in, and Betteredge introduced me to her. A moment later, a thin girl came limping into the room.

'Mr Betteredge,' she said, 'tell me his name again.'

'Mr Franklin Blake,' answered Betteredge.

The girl turned and suddenly left the room. In a second she was back, a letter in her hand, signalling to me to come outside!

I followed her down the beach. She led me behind some boats, and then stopped, and faced me.

I could not possibly misunderstand the look in her eyes. She hated me.

'Take this letter,' she exclaimed furiously, pushing it into my face, 'and I hope I shall never see you again!'

She went back up the beach as fast as she could.

The envelope contained Rosanna's letter, and another a piece of paper. I read the letter first:

> *Sir, — If you want to know the meaning of my behaviour to you while you were staying in the house of my mistress, Lady Verinder, do what you are told to do in the note that comes with this letter — and do it alone. Your humble servant, Rosanna Spearman.*

I looked at the small piece of paper next. Here is a copy of it:

> *Go to the Shivering Sand when the tide is out. Walk out on the South Spit, until you can see the South Spit Signal and the flagstaff at the Coastguard station above Cobb's Hole in a line together. Lay down a stick to guide your hand, exactly along that line. You will touch a chain there. Feel along the chain, until you come to the part which stretches over the edge of the rocks, into the quicksand. Then pull the chain.*

When Betteredge saw the letter and the note, he said excitedly that Sergeant Cuff had been sure Rosanna had hidden something which would explain the mysterious theft. The tide would go out in an hour. We had plenty of time to reach the quicksand.

The tin case

We were soon walking out on the South Spit. I stood in the right position to see the Signal and the Coastguard flagstaff in a line together. I laid my stick in the necessary direction on the rocks.

5

I felt along the stick until I my fingers touched a chain, but then I found my hand stopped by a thick growth of seaweed. I could not pull up the seaweed, or push my hand through it. I decided to try to find the chain at the point where it entered the quicksand with my stick. At the first attempt, the stick struck the chain! I pulled it. Moments later, I held a tin case in my hands.

I pulled off the lid, and drew out a roll of white linen. There was also a letter in the case, which I put in my pocket. When I was back on the beach, I unrolled the linen. It was a nightgown, and it was marked with paint from the door in Rachel's sitting room!

I remembered Sergeant Cuff saying that if there was an article of clothing in the house with a paint stain on it, and its owner had no reasonable excuse for it, then that person was very likely the thief. I had discovered the marked clothing, but to whom did the nightgown belong?

Then I remembered that the nightgown was probably marked with its owner's name. I picked it up, and looked for the name.

I found it — it read *Franklin Blake*. I was the thief!

Rosanna's letter

I felt sick and weak. Betteredge hurried over to me and
I gave him the nightgown. I told him to read the name.
He was as shocked as I was.

5   We went back to Betteredge's room, and after some
brandy I began to feel better.

'Well, Betteredge, I have to admit that this is my
nightgown,' I said at last.

'Somebody is trying to put the blame on you, sir!' said
10   Betteredge. 'Was there nothing else in the tin case?'

I remembered the letter and opened it. This is what it
said:

*Sir — I have something to tell you. I love you. I shall
be dead, sir, when you read this letter. You will find your*
15   *paint-marked nightgown in my hiding place. You will
want to know how it came to be hidden by me, and why
I said nothing to you about it while I was still alive. I
did these strange things because I loved you.*

I loved you from the first moment I saw you, but you
20   *never noticed me. I began to hate Miss Rachel, because
you spent so much time with her. Dear sir, I was so very
unhappy.*

*When the Diamond was lost, Mr Seegrave sent the
women servants away from Miss Rachel's room. He said*
25   *that one of our dresses had spoiled the fresh paint on the
door. After leaving the room, I stopped on the landing to
see if I had got the paint, by any chance, on my gown.
Penelope Betteredge noticed what I was doing.*

'You needn't worry, Rosanna,' she said. 'The paint on
30   *Miss Rachel's door has been dry for hours. I heard
Mr Franklin say yesterday that it would take twelve hours
to dry. That was at three o'clock in the afternoon. The
door was dry by three o'clock this morning. I left Miss
Rachel in bed at twelve o'clock last night. And I noticed*
35   *the door, and there was nothing wrong with it then.'*

As usual that morning, I started tidying up your bedroom. I picked up your nightgown to fold it, and saw the mark of paint from Miss Rachel's door. I knew it was proof that you were in Miss Rachel's sitting-room between twelve and three.

I did not want you to get into trouble. I decided to keep the nightgown, and to make a new one right away, so that it would not be missed. I had just locked it up in my drawer and gone back to your room, when I was sent for to be questioned by Mr Seegrave.

I met Penelope Betteredge. She was very angry. She said that Mr Seegrave suspected her of being the thief, because she was the last person to be in the sitting-room that night. 'If the last person there is to be suspected,' I thought to myself, 'then the thief is Mr Franklin Blake!'

At last I had a reason to talk to you! I would tell you what I knew, and you would be kind to me.

I went straight to the library where I knew you were writing. You had left one of your rings upstairs, and this was a good excuse for disturbing you.

But, sir, you looked at me coldly, and thanked me for finding your ring, as if you did not care at all. I felt like dying! Then I said, 'This is a strange thing about the Diamond, sir. They will never find it, sir, will they? No! nor the person who took it, I'm sure of that.' I nodded and smiled at you as if to say, 'I know what has happened, and I will do all I can to help you!' You looked interested then, but Mr Betteredge came to the door, and I had to go.

I pretended to be ill at dinner time, so that I could have the afternoon to myself. What I did, I need not tell you. Sergeant Cuff discovered that much.

On the Friday morning the new nightgown was made, marked, and placed in your drawer. I had got the only proof against you. And no one knew it, not even you.

Sergeant Cuff had found out the truth of the marked door. I was sure that he would want to look at our clothing. There was no safe hiding place in the house, so I put the nightgown on. I had just done this, when Sergeant Cuff wanted to see the laundry book.

I took it to him. We had met before, when I was in prison. I was certain he recognized me. I felt that he might arrest me at any moment and have me searched.

Shortly afterwards, all the servants were called to see Sergeant Cuff, one at a time. I could tell by his questions that someone had been listening outside my door on Thursday. The Sergeant knew enough for him to have guessed some of the truth. He thought that I had made a new nightgown, but he wrongly believed the paint-stained gown to be mine. He suspected me of having something to do with the loss of the Diamond, but thought I was helping someone else. You were safe as long as the nightgown was hidden. I was frightened that I might be searched at any moment. I had to choose between destroying the nightgown, or hiding it in a safe place. How could I destroy the only thing I had which proved I had saved you? I decided to hide it at the Shivering Sand.

I went straight to the Yollands' cottage. They were the best friends I had. I wanted to write this letter to you, and to have a chance to take off the nightgown. I shall find what I need for keeping it safe and dry in its hiding place, at Mrs Yolland's. Then I shall go and hide it in the Shivering Sand. I shall speak to you once more. If you are still cruel, I don't want to go on living. Forgive me,

Your true lover and humble servant,

Rosanna Spearman

Betteredge's advice

I decided to go back to London and talk to Mr Bruff, and try and see Rachel.

'Before I go, Betteredge,' I said, 'I have two questions to ask you. First, was I drunk on the night of Rachel's birthday?'

Betteredge thought for a moment.

'Well, sir,' he said, 'we gave you some brandy-and-water, as you looked unwell. But we only put half a wine glass of brandy in it, the rest was hot water. A child couldn't have got drunk on it.'

'When I was a boy, did you ever discover me walking in my sleep?' I asked next.

Betteredge looked at me.

'You're trying to find a reason for getting the paint on your nightgown without knowing it yourself. But as far as I know, you never walked in your sleep in your life.'

I felt that Betteredge's answers must be right. But then how did the paint get onto my nightgown without my knowing it? I must be the thief!

Betteredge saw that I was upset.

'You may have touched the wet paint without knowing it, sir, and taken the Diamond without knowing it. But think what has happened since then. The Diamond has been taken to London and given to Mr Luker in exchange for money. You did not do that without knowing it. Go and see Mr Bruff, sir. Maybe he will help you to see things more clearly.'

WHAT RACHEL SAW

In the music room

When I arrived in London, I drove to Mr Bruff's house. I showed him the nightgown and Rosanna Spearman's letter.

5   'Well, I can understand Rachel's strange behaviour now,' said Mr Bruff. 'She thinks you stole the Diamond. The first thing to do is to talk to her. She must tell us why she believes that you took the Moonstone. If she suspected you on the evidence of the nightgown, the
10 chances are that Rosanna Spearman showed it to her. The disappearance of the jewel gave this girl, a thief herself, an opportunity to part you and Rachel for the rest of your lives.'

    Two days later, Mr Bruff came to see me to say that he
15 had asked Rachel to lunch at his house that day. He had not spoken to her about me. He gave me the key of his garden gate, and told me to let myself in through the garden. At three o'clock I should make my way to the music room. There I would find Rachel — alone.

20   After Mr Bruff had gone, a letter arrived for me from Betteredge. He said Mr Candy had heard I had been to Yorkshire. The old doctor wanted to see me for some special reason, and had asked that I go to visit him next time I was in the neighbourhood.

25   At three o'clock exactly, I was standing outside Mr Bruff's music room, listening to someone playing the piano inside. Then, taking a deep breath, I opened the door. As I went into the room, Rachel rose from the piano stool.

30   We looked at each other in silence. I took a few steps towards her. Slowly, she came towards me, trembling.

I caught her in my arms, and kissed her. For a moment I thought the kiss was returned. Then she pushed me away.

'After what you've done, how could you creep in here to see me like this?' she cried angrily.   5

'What have I done?' I said.

'How can you insult me by asking that question?' she said. 'You, who were once so dear to my mother, and dearer still to me — '

She sat down, and hid her face in her hands.   10

'Please listen,' I said. 'I have something serious to say.'

Then I told her of my discovery at the Shivering Sand. She did not move or speak. I asked her if Rosanna Spearman had shown her the nightgown.

'Are you mad?' she cried, staring at me. 'Have you come   15
here to pay me for the loss of my Diamond? Are you suddenly ashamed of what you have done? Is that the real reason for your story about Rosanna Spearman?'

'You are wrong!' I answered, trembling. 'I have to know the reason why you suspect that I am the thief!'   20

'Suspect you!' she exclaimed. 'You wicked man, I saw you take the Diamond with my own eyes!'

Solving the mystery

'I was so amazed that I could not say a word. I took her by the hand, drew her gently back to her chair, and sat   25
beside her.

'Rachel,' I said. 'I need your help. You saw me take the Diamond, but I swear before God, that I didn't know I had taken it until you told me just now!'

Her head sank onto my shoulder, and she placed her   30
hand in mine.

'I want you to tell me,' I said, 'everything that happened, from the time we said goodnight, to the time when you saw me take the Diamond.'

'Oh, why go back to it now!' she cried.   35

'We must, Rachel! For the sake of our future happiness together, we must try to solve this mystery,' I said. 'Let us begin with what happened after we said goodnight to each other. Did you go to bed immediately?'

5 'I went to bed. It was about twelve o'clock, I think. But I couldn't sleep, so about an hour later I got up and lit my candle. I was going to my sitting-room for a book, and I saw a light under the door, and heard footsteps. I thought it was Mother, coming to speak to me about the
10 Diamond. She was anxious about me keeping it in my cabinet.'

'What did you do?'

'I blew out my candle, so that she would think I was in bed. But I did not go back to bed, for at that moment
15 the sitting-room door opened, and I saw you. You were in your nightgown, and carrying a candle. I saw your face quite plainly. Your eyes were open, and you looked all around you when you came in.'

'What did I do next?'

'You went to my Indian cabinet and took the Diamond out. You stood still, for what seemed a long time. Then you suddenly turned and went out of the room. I didn't go back to my bed that night. Nothing else happened.'

'You stole it!'

I dropped her hand, and rose from my seat.

'If you had spoken when you ought to have spoken,'
35 I began, 'if you had explained to me — '

She interrupted me with a cry of fury.

'In spite of what I had seen, I was so fond of you I could not believe that you were a thief. I couldn't tell anybody. I wrote you a letter.'

'I never received it.'

'I know. My letter said that I hoped that you would return the Diamond secretly. But next morning I heard that it was you who had sent for the police. I was so ashamed and upset that I tore the letter up.'

'If you had spoken to me at the time, you might have found out that you had cruelly wronged an innocent man,' I said.

'If I had told the truth to everyone,' she answered, 'you would have been disgraced. If I had spoken to you, you would not have admitted it, as you are not admitting it now! I don't believe you found the nightgown, or Rosanna Spearman's letter, I don't believe a word you have said. You stole it — I saw you! You took it to the money-lender in London! You ran off to the Continent with the money the next morning! Now you come here, and tell me I have made a mistake!'

I passed her and opened the door. She caught my arm.

'Let me go, Rachel,' I said. 'It will be better for both of us.'

'Why did you come here?' she asked. 'Are you afraid I shall give you away? I can't!' She burst out crying loudly. 'I can't help the way I feel for you, even now!'

'You shall know that you have been mistaken about me,' I said. 'Or you shall never see me again!'

With those words, I left her.

I want to clear my name

Later that evening Mr Bruff paid me a visit. He said he had just taken Rachel home. She had told him everything, and was very upset. I told him that I would not ask to see her again. Mr Bruff nodded.

'We can hardly blame Rachel for believing that you are guilty. Let us think of what we can discover to explain your actions. Now, it is already June. At the end of the month someone will pay back the money he borrowed from Mr Luker, and the Diamond will be returned. Mr Luker must go himself to collect it from the bank. I will employ someone to watch the bank, and find out who Mr Luker gives the Diamond to. That person alone can put things right between you and Rachel.'

This was a clever plan. However, I wanted to clear my name as soon as possible. I decided to go and see Sergeant Cuff. Early next morning I travelled to Dorking — the place where Sergeant Cuff was now living. Unfortunately, he had just gone on holiday. I left a message, asking him to please write to me as soon as he returned.

When I got back to London, I thought over and over again about the day of the party at my aunt's house. Had anything important happened when we all sat down to dinner? I decided to ask all the people who had been at the party, to tell me what they could remember.

Mr Bruff told me that Mr Murthwaite was again in Asia and Miss Clack was living in France. However, Mr Godfrey Ablewhite might be somewhere in London. I could ask at his Club.

I drove to Godfrey's Club, but he wasn't there. I found out that after Rachel had broken off their engagement, he had proposed to another wealthy young lady. That engagement had also suddenly been broken off. Soon after that, an old lady who died had left him five thousand pounds. He had left the day before for the Continent, and would be away at least three months.

Mr Candy is very changed

I then decided to talk to my relatives, the Ablewhites, and to Mr Candy. The doctor had asked specially to see me, so I made the long journey back to Frizinghall, and went to see him first.

I was quite surprised at the change I saw in him. His eyes were dim and his hair had turned completely grey. His memory was now so bad that although he knew he had wanted to see me for some reason, he couldn't remember what it was. I tried to help him by mentioning my aunt's party. 'That's it!' he cried, but what he had wanted to say about the dinner, he just could not remember.

After half an hour, I rose to leave. I felt that Mr Candy had something important to say if only he got his memory back. At the bottom of the stairs I met his assistant, Ezra Jennings. He was the strangest man I'd ever seen. He was tall and thin. His brown eyes were dreamy and sad. His thick curly hair was black in colour on the top of his head, but around the sides it had turned snow white.

The doctor's assistant was on his way to see a patient, and we left the house together. I told Ezra that Mr Candy had been trying to speak to me of something that had happened before he was taken ill.

'His memory of things which happened before is very poor,' said Ezra Jennings.

'I must know what it is he wants to say,' I said. 'Isn't there any way to help him get his memory back?'

The notes

Ezra Jennings looked at me strangely.

'Nothing can bring back Mr Candy's memory, but I may be able to tell you what it is he is trying to remember,' said the assistant slowly. 'For some years, I have been writing a book on the brain. In cases of high fever, the patient often says things without knowing it. The words and phrases do not appear to be connected together. I wanted to prove that, in spite of this, the patient was still thinking clearly during his illness. So when Mr Candy fell ill, I sat beside his bed, and wrote down everything he said.

'Nothing made any sense until I added words and phrases of my own that I thought connected Mr Candy's words sensibly.'

'Did he speak of me?' I interrupted eagerly.

'Mr Blake, for a whole night, Mr Candy's mind was occupied with something between himself and you.'

'Why, let me look through your notes,' I cried.

At first he did not want me to see the notes, because of the way he had got the information from a sick man. I then told him the whole story about the Diamond, and how I was suspected of having stolen it.

'It is certain that I took the Diamond,' I said. 'I can only declare that I did it without knowing it myself.'

Ezra Jennings caught me excitedly by the arm.

'Stop!' he said. 'Have you ever needed to use the drug opium?'

'I have never tasted it in my life.'

'Were you unusually restless and bad-tempered, at this time last year?'

'Yes, I had just given up my cigars. Many nights I never slept at all.'

'Was the night of the birthday any different? Try and remember. Did you sleep well that night?'

'I do remember! I slept very well.'

He dropped my arm, and looked at me very seriously.

'I am absolutely certain, Mr Blake,' he said, 'that I can prove that you did not know what you were doing when you took the Diamond. I believe I have the evidence of your innocence.'

Laudanum

We went into Ezra Jennings's study. He handed me his notes, but before I could read them, he asked me some rather strange questions.

'You have already told me that at this time last year, you were nervous and bad-tempered, and you slept badly at night, due to your suddenly giving up smoking. And you have told me that you had a very good night's sleep the night of the theft.'

I nodded, puzzled.

The assistant continued.

'Now, did you and Mr Candy have any kind of argument at the birthday dinner?'

'Yes, we argued about whether or not I should use medicine to calm my nerves.'

'Were you worried about the Diamond, at that time?'

'I was. I knew of the plot connected with it, and I feared for the safety of Miss Verinder.'

'Did anyone mention the safety of the Diamond immediately before you went to bed, on the birthday night?'

'My aunt and Miss Verinder were talking about it.'

'Mr Blake,' said Ezra Jennings, 'you may now read those notes I gave you. You will find that, because of opium, you entered Miss Verinder's sitting-room and took the Diamond, as in a dream. The opium was given to you in a liquid form — known as laudanum, by Mr Candy, without your knowing it. He did it in order to win his argument with you. If he had not become ill, he would have returned to Lady Verinder's the next morning, and told you of his trick. Miss Verinder would have heard of it, and the truth would have been discovered in a day.'

'How was it done?' I asked, amazed.

'I don't know. The opium was given to you secretly in some way.'

I looked at the notes, and this is what I read:

... Mr Franklin Blake has not been sleeping well. I tell him that his nerves are bad, and that he ought to take medicine. He tells me that taking medicine will do him no good at all. I say to him that nothing but medicine can help him find the sleep he needs.

I can give him a night's rest. I know where to find Lady Verinder's medicine chest. I shall give him a small amount of laudanum tonight, without his knowing it. Then I shall call tomorrow and say:
5   *'Well, Mr Blake, you have had a good night's rest. You had a dose of laudanum before you went to bed. What do you say about medicine now?'*

I handed the papers back to Ezra Jennings.

'I believe,' he said, 'that the dose of laudanum caused you to behave as you did on the night of Miss Verinder's birthday.'

'I am sure that you are right,' I agreed.

Ezra Jennings's plan

15   Ezra Jennings thought carefully for a few moments. Then he looked me straight in the eyes. 'Are you willing to try an experiment?' he asked.

'I will do anything to clear myself from suspicion.'

'Mr Blake,' he declared, 'you shall steal the Diamond for the second time without knowing it. This time there will be witnesses.'

I jumped to my feet, and looked at him in surprise.

'Here is my plan,' he said. 'I see you have taken up smoking again. Will you give it up suddenly as you did before?'

'I will give it up from this moment.'

'If, as I hope, the same thing happens as last time, we shall be able to start the experiment. If we can make everything like it was at this time last year — your sleepless nights, your worry about the Diamond — I believe that another dose of laudanum may make you act in the same way.'

'I don't understand the effect that the opium had on me,' I said then. 'I thought that opium was used to make people sleep.'

'That is a mistake often made about opium, Mr Blake! In most cases, it makes a person more active at first, and sends him to sleep later. The worry you felt about the safety of the Diamond would make you do something to save it, then later you would fall into a deep sleep. When morning came, the effect of the opium would have worn off, and you would wake up, remembering nothing that you had done during the night.'

A second dose of laudanum

'You have shown me how I entered Miss Verinder's room,' I said, 'and how I took the Diamond. But she saw me leave with the Diamond too! Can you guess what I did next?'

'The experiment I suggested to clear your name may also help us find the lost Diamond,' he answered. 'You may have hidden it somewhere in your room, and the second dose of laudanum might help you to remember where it is.'

'Impossible! The Diamond is, at this moment, in London.'

'Have you any evidence that the Moonstone was taken to London?' he said. 'Have you any proof that the jewel was pledged to Mr Luker? His banker's receipt was for "a valuable of great price", and he says he has never heard of the Moonstone. The Indians think Mr Luker is lying, and you think the Indians are right. No, Mr Blake, I say that the Diamond is somewhere in the house.'

'Can I write to Mr Bruff, to tell him what you say?' I asked.

'I don't mind at all. Now let us make plans for our experiment. We have decided that you will give up smoking. The next thing to do is to try to get things in the house, as near as possible, the same as they were last year.'

It was impossible to get together all the people who had been in the house last time I slept in it. This didn't bother Ezra Jennings, but he thought the same objects should be around me. I should sleep in the same room and the furniture must be the same as it was then. The stairs, the passages, and Miss Verinder's sitting-room should all look the way they were one year ago.

'Who is going to ask Miss Verinder's permission?' I asked. 'I can't.'

'In that case, I will write to Miss Verinder, telling her of everything we have talked of today.'

I thanked him for all his help, and left the house.

It was then the fifteenth of June. The events of the next ten days are written in the diary kept by Ezra Jennings.

10

THE EXPERIMENT

Miss Verinder believes Mr Blake is innocent

15th June 1849 — I posted my letter to Miss Verinder.

16th June — When I went to see Mr Franklin Blake, I found him very pale. 'I had a restless night,' he said. 'I didn't sleep at all. Exactly like last year, when I stopped smoking my cigars.'

17th June — This morning I received a charming letter from Miss Verinder. She tells me that she is satisfied that Mr Franklin Blake is innocent. She is angry with herself, for not having guessed the truth of the mystery. It is plain that she has loved him all the time.

She asks me not to show Mr Blake this letter. I am only to tell him that she agrees to her house being used for the experiment. She wants to tell him the rest herself, before he is put to the test. I don't think this is a good idea. It might upset our plans, if they were to meet before the experiment.

Mr Blake has had another bad night. He has not yet heard from Mr Bruff. I told him what Miss Verinder had said.

Five o'clock — I have written to Miss Verinder, and have told her that she cannot see Mr Blake before the start of the experiment. I have suggested that she should arrive at the house secretly, on the evening when we make the attempt. I shall see Mr Blake safely into his bedroom. Miss Verinder will stay in her own rooms until the time comes for the laudanum to be given. Then she can watch with the rest of us.

18th June — Mr Blake slept badly again. He had a letter from Mr Bruff, saying he does not agree with what we plan to do. Also he is sure the Diamond was pledged to Mr Luker.

Gabriel Betteredge has promised to arrange the house in the same way as it was at this time last year.

19th June — Miss Verinder has written, agreeing to everything I proposed. The lady with whom she is staying, Mrs Merridew, will accompany her to Yorkshire.

Plenty of witnesses

20th June — Mr Blake is beginning to feel ill because of his bad nights. On our way to the house, he told me he had received a letter from Sergeant Cuff, who will be returning to England in less than a week. I advised Mr Blake to write to him, telling him all that had happened since he gave up the case, and asking him to be present at the experiment. He would be a valuable witness, and his advice might be of great importance in the future if I am wrong about the Diamond being in Mr Blake's room.

21st June — Mr Blake has had the worst night yet. I have had to give him some medicine. I want to be sure he is well enough to try the experiment when the time comes.

22nd June — Mr Blake slept a little last night. We drove to the house to see if the new furniture had come. Everything will be ready by tomorrow — Saturday. The experiment will be next Monday.

I asked Mr Blake to write to Mr Bruff, asking him to be a witness. He has also written to Sergeant Cuff. With these two, Miss Verinder, and old Betteredge, we shall have plenty of witnesses.

23rd June — Mr Blake is not so well again today.

24th June — Mr Blake was over-excited this morning. If he has another bad night, I am sure our plan will be successful.

25th June — Monday, the day of the experiment! It is
five o'clock in the afternoon. We have just arrived at the
house. Mr Blake is very tired. I believe that the opium
will work exactly as it did last year. Miss Verinder and
Mrs Merridew are travelling by the afternoon train with   5
Mr Bruff.

Nothing has been heard of Sergeant Cuff. No doubt he
is still in Ireland.

We are going to have our dinner at exactly the same
time as the birthday dinner was given last year. After   10
dinner, I shall start talking about the Moonstone, and the
Indian plot to steal it. Then I shall have done all I can to
help Mr Blake, before the time comes to give him the
laudanum.

The experiment   15

Ten o'clock — I have found, in the medicine chest, the
laudanum which Mr Candy used last year. I am going to
use the same mixture. The witnesses reached the house
an hour ago.

Just before nine o'clock, I persuaded Mr Blake to go to   20
his bedroom. I went with him. I had arranged that Mr Bruff
should be in the next room. A short time afterwards, I
heard a knock at the door. I went out, and met Mr Bruff
in the corridor. Miss Verinder had arrived.

I went to Miss Verinder's sitting-room and she ran to   25
speak to me. She shook my hand.

'I can't treat you like a stranger,' she said. 'How happy
your letters have made me!'

She looked at my ugly face, with such a sweet smile.
She was so kind and beautiful.   30

'Where is he now?' she asked excitedly. 'What is he
doing? When will you give him the laudanum? May I see
you pour it?'

She spoke to me as she might have spoken to a
brother.   35

'You have given me a new life,' she said. 'I love him — I have loved him all the time. When tomorrow comes, and he knows I am here, do you think — ?'

She stopped and looked at me eagerly.

'When tomorrow comes,' I said, 'I think you have only to tell him what you have just told me.'

I went to see Mr Blake. He was walking about restlessly.

'Where is Mr Bruff?' I asked.

He pointed to the closed door between the two rooms. Mr Bruff had been in for a few moments, and had said again how useless he thought this experiment would be. Then he had gone to his room, to read some professional papers.

'When are you going to give me the laudanum?' asked Mr Blake impatiently.

'You must wait a little longer,' I said. 'I will stay with you until the time comes.'

Two o'clock a.m. — The experiment has been tried.

At eleven o'clock I rang the bell for Betteredge, and told Mr Blake he could get ready for bed.

Mrs Merridew had gone to bed. I told Betteredge to take the medicine chest into Miss Verinder's sitting-room. Then I knocked at Mr Bruff's door.

'I am going to prepare the laudanum,' I said, 'and I must ask you to come and watch. You will return here with me, and see me give him the dose. Then I must ask you to remain in the room to see what happens.'

'Very well!' he said. 'I can read my papers anywhere.'

He followed me out of the room, his papers in his hand.

We found Miss Verinder waiting for us. At a table in the corner of the room stood Betteredge with the medicine chest. Mr Bruff sat down, and began to read his papers.

Miss Verinder drew me aside.

'How long will it be before anything happens?'

'It's not easy to say. An hour perhaps.'

'I shall wait in my bedroom, just as I did before. I shall keep the door a little way open. I will watch the door of the sitting-room, and the moment it opens, I will blow my candle out. It all happened that way, on my birthday night.'

I knew I could trust her.

Mr Blake takes the opium   5

I asked Mr Bruff to leave his papers for a moment and watch what I was about to do. He got up, and followed me to the medicine chest. I poured the laudanum into a glass.

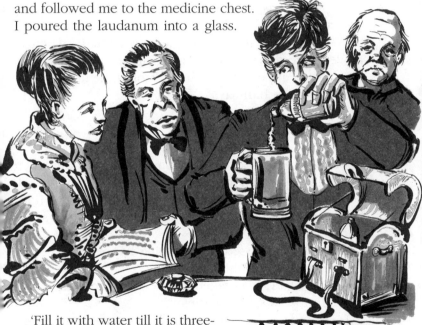

'Fill it with water till it is three-quarters full,' I said, and handed it to Miss Verinder. I then gave her the piece of glass which was to represent the Diamond.

'You must put this where you put the Moonstone,' I said.   15

She put the false Diamond into the cabinet drawer. Then I led the way out, with the laudanum and water in my hand.

'I will wait in my bedroom,' she said.

She closed the sitting-room door behind us. Followed by Mr Bruff and Betteredge, I went back to Mr Blake's room.

In the presence of the two witnesses, I gave him the laudanum, and told him to lie down quietly and wait.

In a part of the room, out of his sight, I placed Mr Bruff and Betteredge to watch the result. I placed a lighted candle on a little table beside the bed, and then sat on a chair at the bottom of the bed.

Mr Blake was restless. I encouraged him to talk to me about the Diamond. We spoke of his taking it from London to Yorkshire; of the danger he had been in when he moved it from the bank at Frizinghall that day; and of the unexpected appearance of the Indians at the house on the evening of the birthday.

The effect of the opium

About twelve o'clock the opium began to work. There was a gleam in his eyes, and he became quite excited. He kept talking about the Moonstone, but he did not finish his sentences. Then there was a silence. At last he sat up in bed.

Ten minutes passed, and nothing happened. Then he suddenly threw off the bed-clothes.

'I wish I had never taken it out of the bank,' he said to himself. 'It was safe in the bank.'

He got out of bed, and walked slowly to the other end of the room. He turned, waited, came back to the bed.

'It's not locked up,' he said. 'It's in her drawer! Anybody might take it. The Indians may be in the house.'

He looked about. After a moment he took up the candle, opened the door, and went out.

We followed him along the corridor, and down the stairs. He never looked back, he never hesitated. He opened the door of the sitting-room, and went in, leaving the door open behind him. He walked to the middle of the room, with the candle still in his hand, and looked about him.

I saw the door of Miss Verinder's bedroom standing open a little way. She was there behind it, hidden in the dark, not saying a word or moving. Mr Blake went straight to the Indian cabinet. He opened one drawer after another, until he came to the one into which the false Diamond had been put. He took out the Diamond, walked back a few steps, and stood still.

So far, he had repeated exactly what he had done on the night of the birthday. Would he show us what he had done with the Diamond when he returned to his own room?

He put his candle down on a table, and wandered towards the sofa, then returned to the centre of the room. I could now see his eyes. They were heavy with sleep. After a minute or two he let the false Diamond drop out of his hand. He did not try to pick it up.

He walked back unsteadily to the sofa, and sat down. Next moment, he was asleep. The experiment was over.

Where is the real Diamond?

I entered the room with Mr Bruff and Betteredge.

'He will probably sleep for the next six or seven hours, at least,' I said.

Miss Verinder came to the door of her room, with a light and a blanket. In five minutes, I had laid him comfortably on the sofa, with the blanket covering him. Miss Verinder wished us goodnight, and closed the door. We three then sat down at the table.

'The first reason for the experiment which was tried tonight,' I said, 'was to prove that Mr Blake entered this room and took the Diamond, last year, acting under the influence of opium. This we have done. The second, was to try to find out what he did with the Diamond. This, we have not been able to do.'

I gave Mr Bruff a pen and paper, and asked him to write down, and sign, a statement of what he had seen that night.

'I beg your pardon, Mr Jennings,' he said, 'for having doubted you. You have been of great help to Mr Blake.'

He wrote and signed the statement. Betteredge signed it too.

'One word about the Diamond,' said Mr Bruff, as we rose from the table. 'I am still sure that it is in Mr Luker's bank in London. I am having the bank watched until the last day of the month. I know Mr Luker must go to get the Diamond himself. If and when he does collect it, I shall have him followed and find out to whom he gives the Moonstone. I am going back to London on the morning train. I shall tell Blake, as soon as he wakes, that he must come with me.'

Mr Bruff shook hands with me, and left with Betteredge.

I went to look at Mr Blake. He lay in a deep, quiet sleep.

While I was looking at him, I heard the bedroom door open. Miss Verinder came towards me.

'Let me watch him with you,' she whispered.

She sat down next to the sofa, and looked at him happily.

I took out my diary, and wrote in it what is written here.

It is just eight o'clock. He is beginning to move. When he opens his eyes, the first person he will see will be Miss Verinder.

I shall leave them together.

11

THE THIEF

Mr Luker goes to the bank

I woke, on the morning of 26th June, not knowing anything of what I had done under the influence of the opium.

I do not feel I need to describe in detail what happened ⁵ after my waking, when, to my great surprise, I found myself in Rachel's sitting room, and Rachel looking lovingly into my eyes. All that needs to be said is that dear Rachel and I understood each other once more. At breakfast, Mr Bruff suggested returning to London by the ¹⁰ morning train. We agreed to travel with him.

When we arrived in London, a small boy met Mr Bruff at the railway station. After listening to him, Mr Bruff asked Rachel and Mrs Merridew to excuse us from going back with them to Portland Place. Mr Bruff then hurried me to ¹⁵ a cab. The small boy sat with the driver, who was told to go to Lombard Street.

'News of Mr Luker,' said Mr Bruff. 'An hour ago, he was seen leaving his house with two police officers in plain clothes. He is going to take the Diamond out of the bank.' ²⁰

'Are we going to the bank?' I asked.

'Yes. Did you notice my boy, sitting by the driver? They call him "Gooseberry" at the office because of his large eyes. He often takes messages for me and is one of the cleverest boys in London. He sees everything.' ²⁵

The cab drew up at the bank. We went in, followed by Gooseberry. The outer office was crowded with people. Two men came up to Mr Bruff to say that Mr Luker had gone into the inner office half an hour ago.

I looked round at the people near me, but I couldn't
see the three Indians anywhere. The only dark-skinned
person there looked like a sailor.

'They must have their spy here somewhere,' said
5 Mr Bruff, looking at the dark sailor suspiciously. 'Ah, here
is Mr Luker!'

The money-lender came out from the inner office,
followed by the two policemen in plain clothes.

'Keep your eyes on Luker,' whispered Mr Bruff. 'If he
10 is going to give the Diamond to someone, he will do it
here.'

Mr Luker walked slowly to the door, his guards on
either side of him. They went out, followed by one of
Mr Bruff's men. I looked round to see where Gooseberry
15 was, but he had disappeared.

An unexpected visitor

We had a meal at Mr Bruff's office. Before we had finished,
the man who had followed Mr Luker came in to see us.

Mr Luker had gone back to his own house and had sent
20 the guard away. He had not gone out again. Our men had
been watching the street in front of the house, and a lane
at the back. No one had been seen behaving suspiciously.

'Do you think Mr Luker has the stone at home?' I asked.

'No,' said Mr Bruff. 'He would never have sent the
25 policemen away if he had decided to keep the Diamond
in his house.'

We waited another half hour for Gooseberry, but he did
not come. It was time for Mr Bruff to go to Hampstead,
and I had to see Rachel in Portland Place. I left my card
30 with the watchman at Mr Bruff's office. I wrote on it that
I would be home at half past ten that night.

Whenever I was with Rachel, I lost all sense of time. I
got home at half past twelve, not half past ten. There was
a message from Gooseberry. He said he would come back
35 in the morning.

At half past nine the following morning, I heard steps outside my door.

'Come in, Gooseberry,' I called out.

'Thank you, sir,' answered a deep voice. The door opened, and I jumped to my feet. It was Sergeant Cuff! 5

'I thought I would call here, Mr Blake, on the chance that you were in town,' he said. 'When I got back last night, I read your letter. Tell me, what has happened since you wrote to me?'

I told him of the experiment with the opium, and of 10 what had occurred at the bank.

'I don't believe that you hid the Diamond,' said the Sergeant, 'but I agree with Mr Jennings that you must have taken it back to your room. Have you any idea what you did with it?' 15

'None at all.'

Sergeant Cuff got up, and went to my writing-desk. He came back with a closed envelope, addressed to me.

'I suspected the wrong person last year,' he said. 'I may be wrong now, too. Wait until you know the truth before 20 you open this. And compare the name of the guilty person with the name I have written in the letter.'

Gooseberry arrives

I put the letter in my pocket. Just then, Gooseberry arrived, and I introduced him to Sergeant Cuff. 25

'Come here, my lad,' said the Sergeant, 'and let's hear what you have to say. You disappeared from the bank yesterday. What were you doing?'

'If you please, sir,' answered the boy, 'I was following a tall man with a big black beard, dressed like a sailor. I 30 saw Mr Luker give him something.'

'Why didn't you tell Mr Bruff what you saw?'

'I hadn't time, sir, he went out in such a hurry.'

'Well?' went on Sergeant Cuff, 'and what did the sailor do, when he got out into the street?' 35

'He called a cab, sir.'

'And what did you do?'

'Held on behind the cab, sir, and ran after it.'

Before the Sergeant could continue, the head clerk from Mr Bruff's office knocked on the door. I went into another room to speak to him. Mr Bruff was not well, he told me, and had to stay indoors. I wrote a letter, telling him of Sergeant Cuff's visit, and that we were now talking to Gooseberry. I promised to let him know whatever might happen later in the day.

I went back to Sergeant Cuff, and found him very excited.

'There's no doubt that this boy has followed the right man,' he said. 'We must go and see what he has found out for ourselves.'

Five minutes later, Sergeant Cuff, Gooseberry and I were in a cab, on our way towards the City.

Gooseberry's story

'One of these days,' said the Sergeant, pointing to Gooseberry, 'that boy will make a very good policeman. He is the cleverest little lad I have met for a long time. I'll tell you what he told me, while you were out of the room.

'The cab, with the boy behind it, went to the Tower Wharf. The sailor got out, and spoke to an officer of the Rotterdam steamboat, which will be leaving this morning. He asked if he could go on board at once.

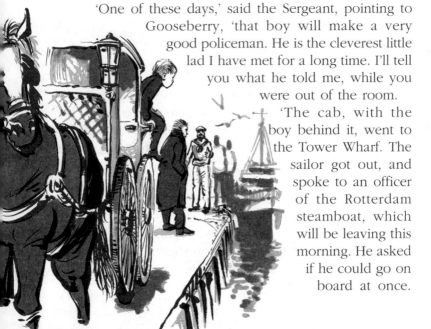

The officer said no. The sailor left the wharf. When he got into the street again, the boy noticed a man dressed like a respectable workman, walking on the opposite side of the road. The sailor stopped at an eating-house, and went in. The other man waited outside. After a minute, a _5_ cab came by slowly, and stopped where the workman was standing. A person in the cab leaned forward to speak to him. That person had a dark face. He might have been Indian. After a while, the cab moved on down the street. The workman crossed the road, and went into the eating- _10_ house. The boy followed him. He saw the sailor at one table, and the workman at another.

'When evening came, the sailor left the eating-house. He didn't notice the boy as he walked past him. The sailor walked on, and the workman soon got up to follow him. _15_ The boy followed them. He saw the sailor go into a public house called The Wheel of Fortune, and he went in too.'

Drunk or sober?

'The sailor asked if he could have a bed for the night. A waiter was sent for to show him to room number ten. Just _20_ before that, Gooseberry had noticed the workman among the people at the public house. Before the waiter had arrived, the workman had disappeared. The sailor was taken up to his room. Then angry voices were heard upstairs. The workman appeared again, this time with the _25_ owner. To Gooseberry's surprise, the workman seemed to have had too much to drink. He was speaking loudly and noisily, and he couldn't walk well. The owner threw him out of the door, and threatened to call the police if he came back. _30_

'It seemed that the workman had been discovered in room number ten, and had declared that it was his room. Gooseberry was so surprised by the sudden change in the man who had not been drunk before, that he ran out after him. While he was within sight of the public house, _35_ the man continued to walk unsteadily. The moment he turned the corner of the street, he straightened up, and became perfectly sober.

'Gooseberry went back to The Wheel of Fortune. Nothing more was to be seen or heard of the sailor. The workman, however, appeared on the opposite side of the street. He looked up at one particular window, which had a light in it. Then he left the place. The boy made his way to Mr Bruff's office, got your message and called to see you, but you were still out.'

A very serious matter

'What do you think of all this, Sergeant?' I asked.

'I think it is very serious, sir. Judging by what the boy saw, the Indians have something to do with it, for sure.'

'Yes. And the sailor was given the Diamond. The workman was working for the Indians, of course.'

'The workman must have had some instructions from the Indians, Mr Blake. They would want a description of the room the sailor was in: of its position in the house, and of any way of getting into it, from the outside. The man ran upstairs to look at it, before the sailor moved in. He was found there, and he pretended to be drunk, as the easiest way of getting out of trouble. He probably went to see the Indians, and they, no doubt, sent him back to make sure that the sailor was safely settled at the public-house until the next morning.'

A locked door

A quarter of an hour later, our cab stopped at The Wheel of Fortune. The moment we entered the house, it was plain that there was something wrong. Sergeant Cuff asked to see the owner, and was told that he was upstairs and not to be disturbed.

'Come along with me, sir,' said the Sergeant, leading the way upstairs. We met the owner on the first floor. He was a very angry man.

'What do you want?' he asked.

'I am Sergeant Cuff,' said the Sergeant quietly.

The owner took us into a sitting-room.

'Something unpleasant happened this morning,' he said.

'This gentleman and I,' said the Sergeant, 'want to ask you a few questions about a dark sailor who slept here last night.'

'Good God! That's the man who is upsetting the whole house at this moment!' exclaimed the owner. 'He left instructions last night, that he was to be woken at seven o'clock this morning. When he was called, there was no answer, and his door was locked. They tried again at eight, and then at nine. No use! A boy has gone to fetch a carpenter. In a few minutes, gentlemen, we will have the door opened, and see what is wrong.'

'Could the man have left the room without using the door?'

'The room is at the top of the building,' said the owner. 'But there is a trap-door in the ceiling, leading out onto the roof.'

The carpenter arrived, and we all went upstairs at once, to the top floor. I noticed that the Sergeant looked very grave.

The door was opened and we went in.

Murder!

We looked towards the bed. The man lay there, dressed — with a pillow over his face. Sergeant Cuff led the way to the bed, and removed the pillow.

The man's dark face was still. His eyes stared, wide-open, at the ceiling. I turned away, and went to the open window.

'He's dead,' said the Sergeant. 'Send for the police.'

Then a small voice whispered, 'Look here, sir!'

Gooseberry had made a discovery. He led me to a table in the corner of the room.

On the table was a little wooden box, open and empty. On one side of the box lay some cotton wool. On the other side was a torn sheet of white paper, with some writing on it:

> *Left with Messrs Bushe, Lysaught, and Bushe, bankers, by Mr Septimus Luker, of Lambeth, a small, sealed, wooden box, containing a valuable of great price. The box, when claimed, to be given only to Mr Luker himself.*

These lines proved to us that the sailor had been in possession of the Moonstone when he had left the bank on the previous day.

Sergeant Cuff took me to the bedside.

'Mr Blake,' he said, 'this man's face is disguised. Let us see what is under this.'

He seized the black hair with his hand and began to pull at it. I could not bear to look, and turned away from the bed.

'He's pulling off his wig and his beard!' whispered Gooseberry.

There was a pause, and then a cry of surprise. Sergeant Cuff asked for a bowl of water. Gooseberry danced about with excitement.

'Now he's washing his face!'

The Sergeant suddenly came to where I was standing.

'Come back to the bed, sir!' he began. Then he changed his mind. 'No! Open the sealed envelope I gave you first.'

I opened it.

'Read the name, Mr Blake, that I have written inside!'

I read the name he had written. It was — *Godfrey Ablewhite.* Then I went and looked at the man on the bed.

Godfrey Ablewhite!

12

WHAT REALLY HAPPENED

Godfrey Ablewhite's death

Dorking, Surrey

30th July 1849

To Mr Franklin Blake,

Sir, — You will find here answers to your questions, 5
concerning the late Mr Godfrey Ablewhite's death.
1. *Your cousin was killed with a pillow from his bed.*
2. *A small box, with a paper torn from it, was found,*
open and empty, on a table in the room. Mr Luker has
seen the box, and says that it contained the Moonstone. 10
He has admitted giving the box to Mr Godfrey
Ablewhite on the afternoon of 26th June. Clearly, the
stealing of the Moonstone was the reason for the
murder.
3. *A trap-door in the ceiling of the room, which led out* 15
on to the roof, was found to be open. The short ladder,
used for climbing up to the trap-door, was found
placed at the opening. A hole had been cut in the trap-
door. This hole was just behind the bolt which fastened
on the inside. Any person from the outside could have 20
drawn back the bolt, and dropped into the room. A
house down the street was empty, and being repaired.
A ladder was left by the workmen, leading from the
pavement to the top of the house. Anyone might have
used the ladder to climb onto the roof of the public- 25
house.

4. *(a) It is known that the Indians wanted the Diamond.
(b) It is probable that the man looking like an Indian,
whom the boy saw speaking to the man who looked
like a workman, was one of the three Hindu*
5 *performers. (c) It is certain that this workman was seen
keeping a watch on Mr Godfrey Ablewhite all through
the evening of 26th, and later on was found in his
room, and could have been examining it. (d) A piece
of torn gold thread was picked up in the bedroom,*
10 *which is believed to have been made in India. (e) On
the morning of 27th, three men looking like the three
Indians were seen at Tower Wharf. They left London
by the steamboat going to Rotterdam.*

This evidence shows that the murder was committed
15 *by the Indians.*

A two-sided life

*I write next about Mr Godfrey Ablewhite. His life had two
sides to it.*

The side we all knew was that of a very charming
20 *gentleman. He was kind, and fond of helping charity
societies, mainly those run by women. The side of him
that we did not know was that of a man who liked to
enjoy himself. He had a house just outside London, with
a lady living in it who was not his wife. In the house I*
25 *found fine pictures and statues. The lady's jewels are
worth a great deal, and so are the carriages and horses.
All these things were paid for by Mr Ablewhite.*

*Mr Godfrey Ablewhite had been trusted to manage a
large sum of money, twenty thousand pounds, for a*
30 *young gentleman who was still under twenty-one in the
year 1848. The young gentleman was to receive the whole
amount when he became twenty-one, in February 1850.
Until then, an income of three hundred pounds per year
was to be paid to him by his two trustees, at Christmas*
35 *and Midsummer Day. This income was paid by the active*

trustee, Mr Godfrey Ablewhite. The twenty thousand pounds, from which the income was supposed to come, had, however, been used up by Mr Godfrey Ablewhite for his own needs. By 1848 it was all gone.

Mr Godfrey needs money

Now we go forward in time to Miss Verinder's birthday.

On the day before, Mr Godfrey Ablewhite arrived at his father's house, and asked for a loan of three hundred pounds. The payment to the young gentleman was due on 24th, and the whole of his fortune had now been spent by his trustee, Godfrey Ablewhite. Old Mr Ablewhite, however, refused to lend his son any money.

The next day Mr Godfrey Ablewhite rode over to Lady Verinder's house. He proposed to Miss Verinder. If she accepted him, he thought he would have the money that he needed. But Miss Verinder refused him.

On the night of the birthday, Mr Godfrey Ablewhite's position was this. He had to find three hundred pounds by 24th June 1848, and twenty thousand pounds, by February 1850. If he failed, he was a ruined man.

You made Mr Candy so angry at dinner that night that he played a joke on you, by giving you a dose of laudanum. He trusted Mr Godfrey Ablewhite to give you the dose, and this gentleman poured the laudanum into the brandy-and-water that you drank before you went to bed. We know this, because Mr Godfrey Ablewhite confessed to it, as you will soon hear. Mr Bruff and I have been to see Mr Luker. Here is what he had to say.

Late on Friday, 23rd June 1848, Mr Luker was surprised to find Mr Godfrey waiting for him. He was more than surprised when Mr Godfrey produced the Moonstone. Mr Godfrey Ablewhite wanted Mr Luker to buy the gem. Mr Luker tested the Diamond, and said that its value was thirty thousand pounds. Then he asked, 'How did you get this?'

The harmless joke

After several attempts to hide the truth, Mr Godfrey Ablewhite was forced by Mr Luker to tell everything.

5   *When he had put the laudanum into your glass of brandy-and-water, he said good-night to you, and went to his own room. It was next to yours, and there was a door between the two rooms. Just as he was getting ready for bed, he heard you talking to yourself.*

He looked into your room, and saw you with the candle
10   *in your hand, just leaving the bedroom. He heard you say, in a voice unlike your own, 'How do I know? The Indians may be hiding in the house.'*

Until then, he had thought he was helping to play a harmless joke on you. Now the idea came to him that the
15   *laudanum was working on you in some way that the doctor had not expected. He was afraid you might have an accident, so he followed you to Miss Verinder's sitting-room, and saw you go in.*

He not only saw you take the Diamond out of the
20   *drawer; he also saw Miss Verinder, silently watching from her bedroom. He knew that she saw you take it too.*

Mr Godfrey was going back to his bedroom when you

came out. You saw him and called to him in a strange, tired voice. He came back to you. You gave him the Diamond. You said to him, 'Take it back to the bank in Frizinghall. It's safe there — it's not safe here.' You turned away, and sat down in the large armchair in your room. Soon you were asleep. Mr Godfrey went into his own room, taking the Diamond with him.

In the morning, it was clear that, from what you said and did, you had no idea of what had happened. Miss Verinder said nothing. Mr Godfrey kept the Moonstone.

Mr Luker agreed to lend Mr Godfrey Ablewhite the sum of two thousand pounds, on condition that the Moonstone was left with him as a pledge. If, at the end of one year from that date, Mr Godfrey Ablewhite paid three thousand pounds to Mr Luker, he could have the Diamond back. If he couldn't pay the money, the Moonstone would belong to Mr Luker.

Your cousin did not like these conditions, but it was 23rd June, and he needed three hundred pounds to pay the young gentleman on 24th.

He again proposed to Rachel, and this time she accepted. However, soon afterwards he discovered that she wasn't going to have a lot of money from her mother. He therefore did not mind when she later broke off the engagement. He could not get the twenty thousand pounds that way.

His luck changed for the better when an old lady left him five thousand pounds in her will. With this money he was able to get back the Moonstone. If he had managed to get to Amsterdam with it, to have it cut up into separate stones and sell them, there would have been no trouble in finding the twenty thousand pounds that he needed by February, 1850.

There is still a chance that we may catch the Indians, and get back the Moonstone. They are now on their way to Bombay, in a ship called the Bewley Castle. *This ship does not stop at any other port on its way, and the police will be ready to go on board, the moment she enters the harbour.*

I remain, dear sir, your obedient servant,

Richard Cuff
(at one time Sergeant in the Detective Force, Scotland Yard, London).

EPILOGUE

The finding of the Diamond

1. Statement of the Captain of the *Bewley Castle* (1849).
I have been asked by Sergeant Cuff to write what I know
of three men, believed to be Hindus, passengers last
summer on my ship, the Bewley Castle, sailing to Bombay.

The Hindus came on board the ship at Plymouth. Off
the coast of India, our ship had to stop because there was
no wind for three days and nights. The tide took us in
near the land.

At sunset, some of the gentlemen passengers lowered a
few small boats, and amused themselves rowing and
swimming round the ship. The boats were left tied to the
side of the ship.

On the following morning, one boat was missing, and
the three Hindus were reported missing too. If they had
taken the boat just after dark, it was no use trying to
catch them. We were so close to land, that they would
easily have reached it and got away by then.

When we arrived at Bombay, I learnt for the first time
why these passengers left the ship. Since then, nothing
has been heard of them.

2. Statement of Mr Murthwaite, written to Mr Bruff (1850).
Let me remind you, my dear sir, of a conversation we
had together when we met at a dinner in London, in the
autumn of 1848. We talked about an Indian Diamond,
called the Moonstone, and of a plot to get possession of
the gem.

Since that time, I have been travelling in Central Asia.
About a fortnight ago, I found myself in a wild part
of Kattiawar. The people here practise the Hindu religion.

One of the most famous Hindu temples is in the sacred
city of Somnauth. In the eleventh century, this city was
destroyed by the Mohammedan conqueror, Mahmoud.

*As I was only three days' journey away from Somnauth,
I decided to visit it.*

*I started along the road and, after a while, noticed
that other people were travelling in the same direction.
Some of them spoke to me. I pretended that I was a* 5
*Hindu-Buddhist. I know the language quite well, and am
tall, thin and brown. They thought I was a stranger from
another part of their own country. On the second day,
the number travelling in my direction had increased to
hundreds. On the third day, there were thousands. We* 10
were all going towards Somnauth.

*I was told that the crowd was on its way to a great
religious ceremony, which was to be on a hill outside the
city. It was in honour of the Moon god, and was to be
held at night.* 15

The god of the Moon

*By the time we reached the hill, the full moon was high
in the sky. My Hindu friends took me with them. When
we arrived, we found we could not see the temple because
a large curtain hung in front of it between two huge* 20
*trees. Beneath them there was a flat rock platform. We
stood below this.*

*Looking back down the hill, I could see tens of
thousands of people, all dressed in white. Red torches
gleamed from every part of the crowd. The moonlight* 25
shone brightly on us all.

*Suddenly, I heard the sound of music. I turned, and
saw on the rocky platform the figures of three men. One
I recognized as the man to whom I had spoken at Lady
Verinder's house in Yorkshire. One of the people standing* 30
next to me explained why the three men were there.

*They were the priests who had sacrificed their high
position in the service of the god. The god had
commanded that on that night, the three men were to
part. They were to go in separate directions, to visit all* 35

the sacred temples of India. They were never to see each other again. They were to keep travelling until they died.

The music stopped. The three men bowed low on the rock, in front of the curtain which hid the temple. They put their arms around each other. Then they came down among the people. The crowd parted to let them through. Slowly the mass of the people closed together again, and we saw the three priests no more.

The music began again, loud and exciting. The curtain between the trees was drawn aside, and we could see the temple.

There, high on a throne, with his four arms stretching towards the four corners of the earth, was the god of the Moon. And there, in his forehead, gleamed the yellow Diamond, whose beauty I had last seen in England, shining on a woman's dress!

Yes! After eight centuries, the Moonstone looks out once more, over the walls of the sacred city in which its story began.

QUESTIONS AND ACTIVITIES

CHAPTER 1

Put the right description with each name.

1. John Herncastle	2. Gabriel Betteredge	3. Lady Julia Verinder
a) A child of the streets who had been in prison.	b) An army officer who killed three holy men.	c) Lady Verinder's very handsome nephew.
4. Franklin Blake	5. Rosanna Spearman	6. Rachel Verinder
d) The chief servant in Lady Julia's house.	e) Colonel John Herncastle's niece.	f) The youngest of the Herncastle sisters.

CHAPTER 2

Which sentences are true, and what is wrong with the false ones?

1 Franklin Blake decided to give the Diamond to Rachel immediately.
2 Penelope said Rachel had fallen in love with Franklin at first sight.
3 The sight of Rachel made Franklin remember about the Moonstone.
4 Franklin and Rachel began to paint her sitting-room door together.
5 It was easy to see that Franklin was in love with Rachel.
6 He even began smoking cigars because she loved the smell.

Chapter 3

Who said these things? Choose from: **Miss Rachel, Rosanna Spearman, Penelope, Lady Julia, Franklin Blake.**

1 'The Diamond is gone! Gone! Nobody knows how!'
2 'The loss of the Diamond seems to have affected Rachel strangely.'
3 'Neither you nor anybody else will ever find it!'
4 'I think Rosanna knows more about the Moonstone than she should.'
5 'They will never find it, sir, will they? Nor the person who took it.'

Chapter 4

Use these words to fill in the gaps: **noise, previous, locked, suspect, midnight, morning, burning, maids, light, around, knocked.**

It was clear that something made Sergeant Cuff (1) _____ Rosanna. Two of the (2) _____ had not believed that Rosanna was really ill on the (3) _____ afternoon. They had (4) _____ at her door, which was (5) _____, and listened, but they had not heard anyone moving (6) _____ inside. They had seen a (7) _____ under the door at (8) _____, and had heard the (9) _____ of a fire (10) _____ in the room at four o'clock in the (11) _____.

Chapter 5

Who did these things? Choose from: **Duffy, Nancy, Rosanna Spearman, Miss Rachel, the butcher's man.**

1 — bought a piece of plain cotton material in Frizinghall.
2 — got into the carriage and would not speak to Mr Franklin.
3 — was the last person in the house to have seen Rosanna.
4 — had promised Rosanna to post a letter to Cobb's Hole.
5 — said that he had seen Rosanna going towards the seashore.

CHAPTER 6

Find and correct the ten errors in Mr Godfrey's description of his adventure below.

I was leaving a bank at the same moment as a man I knew. Both of us pushed forward to go through the doorway first, and we exchanged a few angry words. When I arrived home, I was asked to go to see a lawyer. I went at once. When I arrived, I was shown into a room full of people, and seized round the legs. I noticed that the arm holding onto me was very pale. Then my eyes and mouth were uncovered, and I was helped up by two men. A third man went through my pockets. I was given some tea, and left there. I was rescued soon afterwards.

CHAPTER 7

Choose the right words to say what Lady Verinder's will was about.

Lady Verinder had done something to (1) **encourage/prevent** someone from marrying Rachel for her (2) **money/beauty**. According to the will, Rachel and her husband would have a (3) **business/house** in London and in Yorkshire. They were not allowed to (4) **manage/sell** them. They would also have a (5) **monthly/yearly** income. They were (6) **allowed/not allowed** to sell any of the shares or property that (7) **reduced/produced** the income.

CHAPTER 8

Put each beginnings of these sentences with the right endings to say what Rosanna's letter to Franklin Blake was about.

1 Mr Seegrave said the paint on Miss Rachel's door had been spoiled	(a) and I made you a new one so that the old one would not be missed.
2 Penelope noticed me look to see if I had got the paint on my gown	(b) and I saw the mark of paint from Miss Rachel's door.
3 She said that the paint had been dry by three o'clock that morning	(c) between twelve and three.

4   Then, when I tidied up your room, I picked up your nightgown

(d) and one of the women servants' dresses had done it.

5   It was proof that you had been in Miss Rachel's sitting-room

(e) and there had been nothing wrong with it at twelve o'clock the previous night.

6   I didn't want to get you into trouble so I kept the nightgown

(f) and she said the paint on the door had been dry for hours.

CHAPTER 9

Who said these things? Choose from: **Ezra Jennings, Miss Rachel, Mr Bruff, Mr Candy, Mr Franklin.**

1   'She must tell us why she believes that you took the Moonstone.'

2   'After all you've done, how could you creep in here to see me like this?'

3   'You shall know that you have been mistaken about me.'

4   'Have you ever needed to use the drug opium?'

5   'I shall give him a small amount of laudanum tonight.'

CHAPTER 10

Put these sentences in the right order to describe Ezra Jennings's experiment. (The first one is done for you.)

1   At eleven o'clock, Jennings told Franklin Blake he could go to bed.

2   At about twelve o'clock the laudanum began to work.

3   She put the glass into the drawer where she had put the Moonstone.

4   He went straight to the Indian cabinet and took the false Diamond.

5   Then Jennings prepared the laudanum while Mr Bruff watched.

6   He opened the door and went downstairs to Rachel's sitting-room.

7 Franklin sat up, then threw off the bed-clothes and got out of bed.

8 Then Jennings, Mr Bruff and Betteredge went to Mr Franklin's room.

9 Next, he gave Miss Rachel the false Diamond, a piece of glass.

10 Jennings gave him the laudanum in the presence of the two witnesses.

CHAPTER 11

Put the letters of these words in the right order to say what happened in the sailor's room.

We went into the sailor's room. The man lay on the bed with a (1) **wiplol** over his face. Sergeant Cuff (2) **meevord** it. The man's (3) **krad** face was still. His eyes (4) **tesrad** at the (5) **ligecin**. On a table in the (6) **renorc** of the room was a little box, open and (7) **tepym**. On one side of it lay a (8) **hetes** of paper with some (9) **twingri** on it. The words (10) **vrepod** that the sailor had been in (11) **snopisoses** of the Moonstone. Sergeant Cuff pulled off the man's wig and (12) **drabe**, and washed his face. It was Godfrey Ablewhite!

CHAPTER 12

Which are the true sentences, and what is wrong with the false ones?

1 Stealing the Moonstone was not the reason for Godfrey's murder.

2 Mr Godfrey had spent a lot of money on a lady who was not his wife.

3 He had been trusted to manage a small sum of money for a young man.

4 But Godfrey had given the money to charity and it was all gone.

5 He saw Franklin take the Diamond and knew that Rachel was watching too.

6 Franklin gave the Diamond to Godfrey so he could take it to Mr Luker.